NEPHILIM

BOOK SIX IN THE ANGEL CHRONICLES SERIES

ESTER LÓPEZ

Writing & Photographic Services LLC

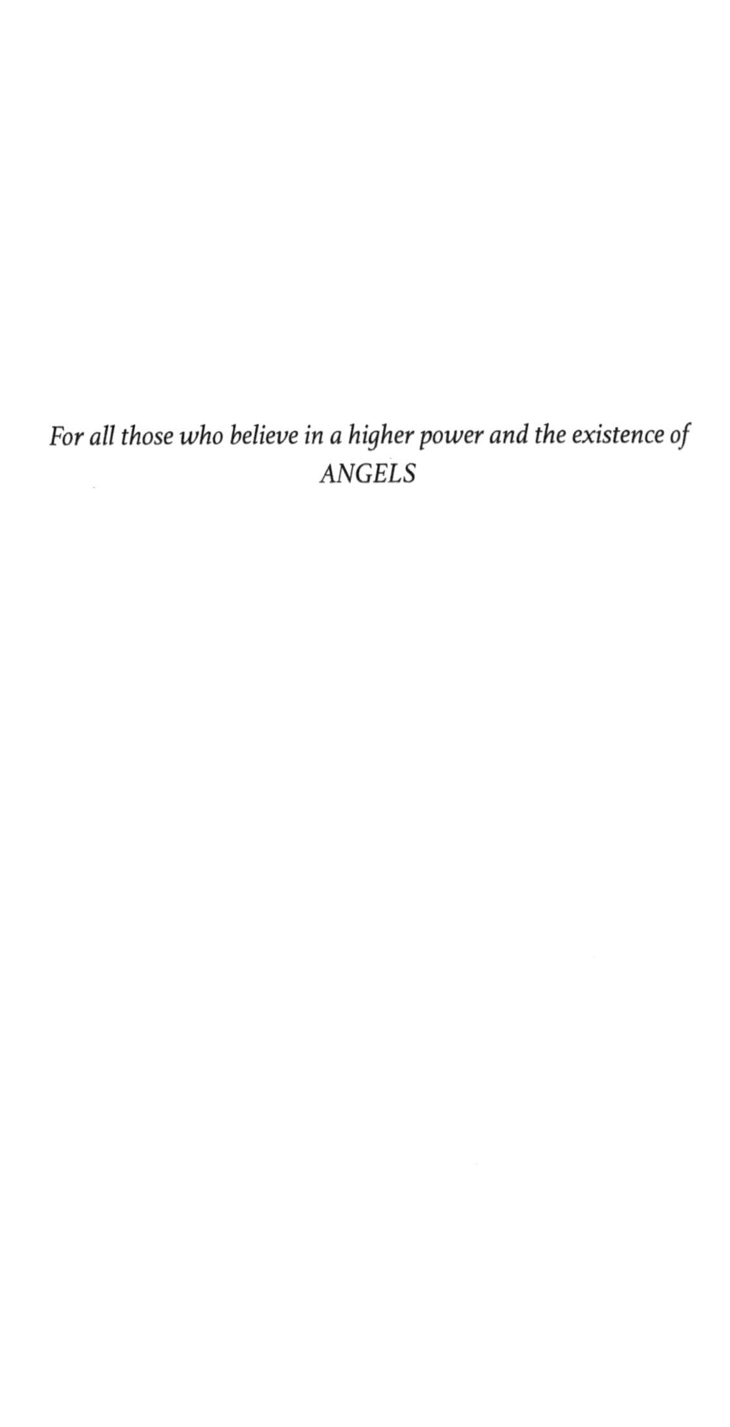

For all those who believe in a higher power and the existence of
ANGELS

PRAYER OF PROTECTION

St. Michael, the Archangel, defend us in battle. Be our Defense against the wickedness and snares of the devil. May God rebuke him, we humbly pray; and do you, Prince of the heavenly host, by the power of God, thrust into hell Satan and all the other evil spirits who prowl about the world for the ruin of souls. Amen.
Most Sacred Heart of Jesus, have mercy on us. (three times)

THE ARMOR OF GOD

Ephesians 6:10-17

Finally, grow strong in the Lord with the strength of his power. Put God's armor on, so as to be able to resist te Devil's tactics. For it is not against human enemies that we have to struggle, but against the Sovereignties and the Powers who originate the darkness in this world, the Spiritual Army of evil in the heavens. That is why you must rely on God's Armor, or you will not have enough resources to hold your ground.

So stand your ground, with truth buckled around your waist, and integrity for a breastplate, wearing for shoes on your feet, the eagerness to spread the gospel of peace, and always carrying the shield of faith so that you can use it to put out the burning arrows of the evil one, and then you must accept salvation from God to be your helmet, and receive the word of God from the Spirit to use as a sword.

1

———

Chapter One

Her name, Noura Hashim, means light destroys evil. And that's what she had done for the last two thousand years. But the times had changed and she had to adjust. When her secret got out, she had to change her name and move to another town, another state, another country, and finally another continent. Her crusade was to stop bullies and fight evil wherever she could. It used to be easy, but with the changing attitudes, it was more difficult to deal with the criminals of each town.

She found herself in Miami. It was the perfect mixture of different races and cultures and she blended in well. She settled down there and changed her name to Alona Gabriel. She bought a small shop and set up business in the downtown area.

With the efficiency of the Miami-Dade Police Department patrols during the day, she felt her business was safe. Her simple way of life kept her away from the criminal elements of society and she was able to live a normal life. It took her a little time to get the word out that she was open for business. Working hard, she was able to make a living. She bought a townhouse and felt as if she belonged here. Soon, her business grew and she hired a young woman to help her. Everything seemed perfect until one day, a demon walked into her shop. She smelled his evil scent before he approached the counter.

"Are you the manager?" he asked.

"Yes. How can I help you?" She really wanted to help him out of her store.

"I'm in the security business and I see you don't have any security systems in place."

"I have my own security system, thank you."

"Really? And what is that?" He placed his hands on her counter. He held a business card in his fingers.

"I don't want to discuss it. Now, if you aren't buying a sandwich, I suggest you leave."

"Very well. I'll leave my card in case you change your mind." He set the card down in front of her.

She glared at him with no expression on her face. Then she watched him slowly leave.

Teresa came up behind her. "Who was that? He was cute. Did you get his number?"

"He was a demon. You don't want to have anything to do with him. Trust me."

Teresa reached for the card.

"Don't touch that!" she shouted.

"What?"

She grabbed a napkin and scooped up the card. She carried it outside to the back trash cans. When she returned, she washed her hands in very hot water and lots of soap.

"What was that about?"

She picked up the sanitizer and sprayed the counter

with it. Then she wiped it down with several paper towels. "It's hard to get a demon scent out of anything," she said. She went back outside with the dirty paper towels and tossed them in the trash receptacle.

"He was just a guy. A very good-looking guy at that. How can you say he was a demon? Did you know him?" Teresa asked.

"No. I can smell a demon. It's a very foul odor. Can't you smell it?"

"No. Are you talking about demons like in Satan and the devils that followed him?"

"Yes. If that's what you want to call him. He was a demon, a devil, an evil spirit in a human form."

"How do you know all this? I mean, he looked like a normal person. He was perfect."

"Yes. Looks can be so deceiving, can't they?"

Teresa looked puzzled.

"There's something about me you don't know." Should she tell her the truth? Would Teresa be able to handle the truth?

"Like what?"

"There are only a few of us who can sense demons or evil spirits. It takes practice, though."

"Yeah, right."

"Have you ever had the sensation that something just doesn't feel right? Or have you had the notion to get away from a certain place?"

"Yes. A time or two, but not many."

"Pay attention to that feeling. If you have it again, run, as fast as you can. And if you ever see that guy again, run like Satan is chasing you. Got it?"

"Sure, sure."

The doorbell chimed as a customer came inside. She

glanced at her watch. 11:30 a.m. Lunch has started. She would let Teresa make the sandwiches until it started hopping, then she would step in and help with the sandwiches. She got here early every day to prep her little kitchen. She had an order coming in today and would handle that herself. Teresa was a good worker. She would eventually teach her everything so she could take time off. Then again, maybe she would just close the shop for a week and they would both be off. It had been a long time since she had a vacation. Being downtown in an office complex, she was able to be closed on the weekends. All the shops were a couple blocks down, and no one came this far on the weekends. This was the perfect little business, and she enjoyed it.

During the day, most of her customers were regulars. She and Teresa chatted with them while making their sandwiches. She took turns with Teresa and let her ring up for a while, while she made the sandwiches.

Finally, it was about three in the afternoon when the food delivery truck came in. Teresa worked the shop, while she checked the items and inventoried everything and put the food away. By the time she finished, it was almost 4:00 p.m. Closing time was 6:00 p.m. Teresa was busy making sandwiches for a pickup.

"How's it going?" she asked.

"We have a couple pickup orders if you want to help me," Teresa said.

"Sure. What've you got?"

Teresa handed her the written order. "I'm finishing up this one."

Before she finished her order, a new customer came in. She did a double take because the guy looked nice. He was taller than her six-foot frame with blondish-brown hair and brown eyes. Hmm. Teresa beat her to him.

"Hello, this your first time here?"

"Does it show?" he asked.

"Well, I haven't seen you in here before, so yes, it does. What'll you have?"

"Hmm, I'll have the number three and a drink."

"Sure thing." Teresa turned toward her.

"I got it, Teresa. You can ring it up."

She hurriedly made the Italian salami, ham, and pepperoni sandwich while Teresa talked to the customer. When she finished, she handed it to him and smiled. She couldn't help it. But she sensed something different about him. Was he a spiritual being? She didn't feel anything negative around him.

"I'll get your drink," Teresa said. She moved past her to get the drink.

"Hi," he said.

"Hi. I'm Alona and I own this shop." She reached her hand out to shake his. His grip was firm, and his hand felt warm and strong.

"Nice to meet you, Alona. I'm Luke. I work down the street at the Martial Arts Academy. Hope you'll stop by some time and check us out."

"I'd love to, thanks."

"Here's your drink." Teresa handed him the drink. "Come back and see us," she said.

"Oh, yes. I'll be back. Thank you, ladies."

She and Teresa watched him walk out.

"Now that's a fine-looking man," she said.

"Yes, he is. Did you get any bad vibes about him?" Teresa asked.

"No, but I did get some vibes."

Teresa stared at her. "What kind of vibes?"

"You know we're all spiritual beings, right?"

"Hmm. I never thought about it."

"Yes. We are all spiritual beings in a human body. He just seems more spiritual than normal."

"Is that good?" Teresa asked.

"If it's what I think it is, it is very good."

Alona closed her sandwich shop about six o'clock and headed to the parking garage with Teresa. It had been a long day, but her shop took in a lot of money, and for that, she was grateful.

She had time to count out the drawer and put the cash into a bank bag she tucked into her purse.

"We did a lot of business this week, didn't we?" Teresa asked.

"Yes. I think it's because of the construction going on down the street." Suddenly, she sensed something was not right and stopped walking. She grabbed Teresa's arm to stop her and motioned with her finger against her lip to be quiet.

Teresa's eyes grew wide, but she remained silent.

A man appeared from behind a column. His hand was in his vest pocket. He pulled out a gun, pointed at the two of them.

"Leave us alone," Alona said.

"I don't think so. What you got in that purse?" he asked.

"None of your business," Alona said. She clutched the purse close to her.

"I'll take your wallets. Both of you," he said.

"No, you won't," Alona said. She glanced at Teresa, who

had reached in her purse. "Don't give him anything!" she said.

"He's got a gun," Teresa whispered.

"He's just a bully," she said.

"I'm not a bully, bitch. I just want your money. Hand it over or you both die," he said.

"Come and get it," she said.

He rushed toward Alona, but she was quicker. She grabbed his throat as he reached for hers, but she grew to over sixteen feet tall. She held his neck with her fingers, while he thrashed and kicked. He dropped his gun while clawing at her hand with both of his hands to free himself.

"Is this what you were planning on doing to me?" she asked.

He grew limp in her hand. She tossed him aside like a rag doll, then shrank to her normal six-foot size.

Teresa stood staring at her. "What are you?"

She took Teresa's arm and turned her to face her. She snapped her fingers in Teresa's face. "Everything you've just seen, you will forget." Then she snapped her fingers again.

"My car is over there," Teresa pointed.

"I'll walk you to your car," she said.

"Thanks, Alona." She opened her car door and climbed inside. "See you tomorrow."

"Tomorrow," she repeated. She headed toward her own car. The city wasn't as safe as she thought it was. Would she have to deal with this again? This was the first time it got violent in a long time. Usually, growing to sixteen feet was all she had to do, and they would run off. But this guy meant to harm them. She could feel the evil surrounding him. He even had the scent of a demon on him. It wasn't strong, but it was there all the same.

She climbed into her car and checked her surroundings

before backing out. She didn't give the scumbag another thought as she drove home. She did go over, in her mind, the new customers she had today. Most of her customers worked in the office complex and nearby buildings. A few came from the construction site down the street. But today, she had a demon stop in the store, and an angel. Were these two entities the ones who had been tracking her the past two thousand years? Would she have to change her name again and move to another continent? She was tired of moving. She wanted to settle down in one place and live a normal life. Was that too much to ask, Lord?

Earlier, she remembered that feeling of foreboding she got, just before the demon showed up. In the past, it would make her paranoid. She ended up moving and changing her ID. Times were different now. Changing an ID and Social Security number was too difficult. Now she had a business to run and that made all the difference. She had settled down in the Miami area because so many people with different nationalities passed through here. She would be able to use all the languages she'd learned over the years.

Finally, she pulled into her subdivision, which was made up of townhouse complexes. Her parking lot had a few cars in it already. It was dinner time, so there would be more people home in the next hour or so. She pulled into her spot and exited her car. Before she unlocked her door, she noticed a blondish-brown dog in the parking lot. They allowed pets here, but she never had one. She hated good-byes and since pets didn't live as long as people, she never got one. This one had beautiful hair coloring. There was something familiar about it, but she couldn't put her finger on it.

The dog moved toward her.

"Hello boy. Where do you belong?"

The dog sat and looked at her as if he understood what she asked. She reached a hand toward the dog, to let him sniff her. "Can I check your collar?" She petted him and realized he didn't have a collar. "I guess you don't have any people, do you?"

The dog cocked his head to the side. "Yeah, me neither."

She went to her neighbor's door on one side and knocked.

"Hello, Mrs. Turner. Do you know whose dog this is?" She pointed to the blondish-brown dog beside her.

"No, I sure don't. I haven't seen him around before. Why don't you try Mr. Johnson. He's home all day. Maybe he knows."

"Sure, thanks." She went to the door on the other side and knocked.

When she asked the same question, Mr. Johnson said, "No. I haven't seen him before. The only ones who have a dog are in the complex across from us. But their dog is a smaller breed."

"Thanks, Mr. Johnson." She glanced at the patient dog beside her. "Well, would you like to have dinner with me?" The dog stood and nodded. "In that case, follow me," she said. She walked toward her door and gestured for him to come in and he did.

She turned on her lights and set her purse down on a table near the entrance and locked the front door. The dog followed her into the kitchen. She pulled containers of leftovers out of the fridge. "I have a lot to choose from tonight, so you're in luck."

After putting the food in microwaveable dishes, she heated them up. While they cooked, she pulled out a bowl and filled it with water. She set it down on the kitchen floor and the dog lapped up the water. Then she served him one dish of food and she took the other. She sat at the bar and gave thanks before she ate her meal. She watched the dog eat all the food.

"It looks like you enjoyed that." She put both dishes in the dishwasher and cleaned up the kitchen. "Let's see what's going on in the world." She walked into the living room, flipping on the tv, and sat on the couch. The dog followed her into the room and sat beside her on the floor.

She petted the dog while the world news was on. "You're pretty clean for a stray dog. What's your name, boy?"

The name Matthias came to her mind. "Is your name Matthias?" The dog wagged his tail and sat up straighter.

This was a first for her. Had he actually spoken to her? Did he understand what she was saying? "Well, Matthias, it's nice to meet you." She reached her hand out and Matthias put his paw into her hand, and she shook it. "Something tells me you're special."

Matthias barked.

"I take that as a yes." She watched Matthias walk to the door and sit. She got up and let him out, walking outside with him. She watched him do his thing. She would have to buy him a collar and leash if she kept him. The small dog park was down the street between two of the complexes. He came back quickly and they both went inside.

The local news was on when she sat back down on the sofa.

"This just in," the news reporter announced. "A body was found late this afternoon in a downtown Miami parking garage. The police are investigating the crime at this hour. We'll have more as it develops."

Her heart skipped a beat. The scene showed the parking garage where she and Teresa were accosted. She sat forward in her seat. A body lay covered in a body bag and crime scene tape was all over the place.

"Oh no!" Her heart pounded. She didn't think about the aftermath of what she had done.

The phone rang moments later, and she jumped.

"Hi Teresa. What's up?"

"Did you just see the news? That was our parking garage. Oh my God, Alona. We were there this afternoon. That could have been us."

"Well, just be thankful it wasn't us. I'm sure they will have security after this."

"I hope so."

"Don't give it another thought. Otherwise, you won't get any sleep. The police will do their job, and everything will be fine."

"Maybe we should start carrying guns," Teresa said.

"They are too heavy to put in my purse. I'll take my chances without one." She hoped Teresa would drop the subject. At least she didn't remember anything, and that was good. "I'll see you tomorrow, Teresa. Have a good night."

The reporter didn't mention cameras, so that was good. She went over the events in her mind. What could she have done differently? The man would have killed both of them. She had all the earnings from the store with her and she wasn't about to let some thug take it. She got up and retrieved her purse, then returned to the sofa. She took the bank bag out and recounted the bills once more. Then she made out the deposit slip. First thing in the morning, she would make a deposit so she could pay each of them for their work this week.

"Well, Matthias, tomorrow I have a deposit to make before heading to work. I hope you have a strong bladder. I'll be gone all day." She leaned over and petted his head. He cocked his head, so she stroked his neck. He seemed to enjoy that, so she continued for a while. "If you decide to stay, I'll have to buy you a leash and some toys." She should probably have him checked by a vet. Maybe she should put an ad in the paper saying she found the dog. While she petted him, she thought of the new customer who came into her shop late in the day. "I met a guy today, Matthias. He was pretty hot. Hopefully, I'll see him again. Your hair color reminds me of him." She got the feeling that after tonight, her life would not be the same.

2

Chapter Two

The next morning, Alona woke up and stretched. Her arm hit something warm, and she jumped. There was Matthias lying in her bed on the pillow next to her, facing her. He opened his eyes and glanced at her.

"Good morning, Matthias! What are you doing in my bed?"

He crawled toward her and lay his head on her stomach. She rubbed his chest. "Don't think this will win you any points, boy." She got up and used the bathroom. Then she slipped on her workout clothes.

"Come on, Matthias, you need to go outside." She walked out with him and waited for him to relieve himself. Once they were inside, she headed to her workout room. She had a routine she did with videos and one with weights. When she was through with that, she fixed breakfast for both of them.

"I'll have to buy you a leash and some dog food today, Matthias."

He raised his head and glanced at her.

"You **do** want to stay, don't you?"

He barked.

"I'll take that as a yes." She cleaned up and then headed to the bathroom to get ready for work. When she stepped out of the shower, she discovered Matthias sitting on her rug, waiting for her. She tried not to step on him while she dried off. Then, while dressing, she noticed him watching her. Since she hadn't had a pet before, she didn't know whether or not this was normal. "We may have to work out different arrangements next time, boy. This bathroom is a little crowded for both of us."

She gathered her purse and the bank bag and set them on the table. She refilled his water bowl. "Okay, Matthias, this is your last trip outside before I head to work." She let him out and watched as he moved around the yard, looking for just the right spot. After he found it, she realized she would need to clean it up before someone stepped in it. When everything was taken care of, she grabbed her things off the table.

"All right." She squatted down. "Now you be a good boy while I'm gone, and I'll see you later." She rubbed his chest, and he licked her face. She stood and grabbed her keys, locking up before heading out the door. While walking to her car, she prayed that Matthias had a good bladder.

~

Matthias stuck his head through the curtains and watched as she drove off. As soon as her car was out of sight, he transformed into Luke. He rubbed his chin and smiled. Then he teleported out of her home.

Alona stopped at the bank and headed on to the shop. She hoped the incident from yesterday was over with. Later, after she closed the shop, she would stop by the grocery store and pick up the dog food and some other things for Matthias.

When she pulled into the parking garage downtown, there was an area to the left that was cordoned off with the yellow crime scene tape. Two officers were stationed on either side of the entrance. Both carried large flashlights and walked toward her car. They stood in front of her car until she came to a stop, then they each walked to her front side windows. The officer on her left motioned to open the window.

"Yes, officer, can I help you?"

"We're investigating a crime here. Do you work in this neighborhood?"

Oh shit! "Yes, sir." *Keep it together, Alona.*

"Did you see anything out of the ordinary yesterday?"

"No, sir." *Breathe, Alona. Just breathe.*

"Do you always park in this garage?"

"Yes, sir. Unless it's full."

She noticed the police officer on her right had walked to the back of her car. Through her rear-view mirror, she saw him pull out a pad and pen and started writing something. *Her license tag! Shit!*

"What happened, officer?" She tried to sound concerned.

"A crime was committed here yesterday. Be careful coming and going from this parking lot," he said.

"Yes sir. May I go now? I have to open my shop."

"Yes. Go ahead." He ushered her forward.

The second police officer stood off to the side now and another car pulled up behind her.

As she pulled forward, the two officers did the same thing to the next car that they did to her. She drove around until she found a parking spot. She gathered her things and headed to the shop. She passed the two officers again as she left the parking lot. They were busy with another car, but they managed to watch her leave.

Once she was inside her shop, she tried to put the incident aside. She put on her apron and pulled her hair back into a ponytail. She washed her hands, then gathered the vegetables she needed for the sandwiches. After all the vegetables were prepped, she prepared the sandwich meats. The last thing she did was set out her breads and wraps she would use. She re-stocked the cups and napkins and turned on her oven and sandwich press. Before she could check the drink machines, there was a knock at the back door.

"Oh my gosh! They were looking for a criminal in our parking lot. Can you believe it?" Teresa said.

"Yes. I was a little late getting here because of that. Did they get your tag number?"

"My license tag?"

She nodded.

"I don't remember."

"Did they tell you what crime was committed?"

"No, but I bet it was that murdered victim from the news last night." Teresa said.

Teresa was right and she knew it. The man had been a thug. He would have killed both of them, if she hadn't stopped him. Certainly, she was justified in what she did. She watched Teresa put on her apron and pull her hair back, while she checked the machines. Then they both washed their hands.

"I'm so glad it's Friday," Teresa said.

"Why, do you have a hot date?" she asked.

"No, but my sister and I are going to the beach tomorrow. Hopefully, we'll meet some hot guys there."

"Good luck with that." She hoped that good-looking man from yesterday came back. She wouldn't mind seeing him again.

"Are you ready? I'm going to open," she said. Alona walked to the front entrance. She flipped on the 'Open' sign and unlocked the door. She stepped out into the morning sunshine and glanced down both sides of the street as she always did. This time, there were several police cars parked at one end. She stood with her hands on her hips. She realized Teresa had joined her.

"Do you think they are going door to door to see if we've seen anything?" Teresa asked.

I hope not! "I really don't know. Why would all these cars be outside the repair shop?"

"Hmm." Teresa shook her head and went back inside.

It was a while before they got busy. The first few orders were by phone for after twelve noon. The first walk-in customers came in after 12:30 p.m.

"Something is off about today," Teresa said.

"I agree."

Mrs. Burns, a regular, came in. "Have you heard the news?"

"No. What's going on with all the police cars?" she asked.

"I have a police scanner in my office. It seems there were

several burglaries reported this morning. One on this block and two on the next."

"No way!" Teresa said. She had finished making Mrs. Burns' order. She handed the sandwiches to Alona. "Who got hit?"

"There was the repair shop and a small appliance store that I remember."

Suddenly, several customers came in at once. Finally, they got busy. After Teresa made the sandwiches, Alona would pack them into bags with their chips and hand them a drink. When there were several orders to go, both women made the sandwiches to speed things up.

Finally, a tall, good-looking man came in with a pretty, Hispanic woman. While Teresa made their sandwiches, the woman asked questions.

"How long has your shop been open?" the woman asked.

"Oh, we've been here about four years now," she said. "I'm Alona Gabriel, the owner. And this is my loyal employee, Teresa."

"Nice to meet you," the woman said.

"You haven't had any trouble here lately, have you?" the man asked.

"No. Why do you ask?" Now she was getting suspicious.

"We just worked three robberies in this neighborhood," the woman said.

"Worked?" she asked. Are these criminals bragging about the robberies? They didn't look like criminals.

The woman pulled out a badge. "We're detectives for the Miami-Dade Police Department."

She glanced at the badge in her hand. It looked official.

"Oh? No. We haven't had any problems." She handed the detective two bottles of water.

"Thank you," the woman detective said. "If you have

anyone asking you about security, would you call us?" she asked.

She hesitated about telling them of her visit by a demon, when Teresa brought up their sandwiches. While the male detective paid, the woman handed her a business card. She watched as the two sat at a table up front, facing the street.

She wondered why they were interested in someone peddling security systems, but more customers came in and she soon forgot about it. The customers slowed down around 3:00 p.m.

"Guess what I found yesterday," she said.

"What?"

"A dog."

"You're kidding? I thought you didn't like dogs," Teresa said.

"It's not that I don't like dogs, it's just that I haven't had time for one in my life. I never thought about it, really. This dog just showed up in the neighborhood yesterday. He didn't belong to anyone, so I took him in."

"Have you had him checked?"

"Checked, like at the vet?"

"Yes. You know, for rabies or diseases and stuff."

"Not yet. I was planning on buying him some dog food and a leash tonight."

"Well, you should have him checked for rabies at least," Teresa said.

"I'll look into it on Monday." Just as she finished talking, the good-looking man from the day before came in.

"Hello," she said. She smiled at him.

"Hello Alona, I'd like to order that same sandwich I had yesterday. The Italian one. It was so good I couldn't stop thinking about it all day."

"Really? I'll be glad to make it for you." She walked over to the counter and Teresa headed to the register.

She quickly put the sandwich together and heard him speaking to Teresa.

"I'm sure you two have heard about the burglaries around here?" Luke said.

"Oh, yes! We even had two cops come in to eat and asked us questions," Teresa said.

"You should think about joining our Marshal Arts Academy. Learning to defend yourselves may come in handy one day." Luke said.

"Do you have a business card?" Alona asked.

"Yes, I do." He handed the card to Alona.

Teresa rung up his sandwich and drink.

"Are you one of the instructors?" Alona asked.

"Yes, I am. Ask for Luke when you call. I'll give you my personal attention." He smiled a sexy smile. She felt her heart skip a beat. She watched as he walked out of the shop.

Teresa punched her hard in the arm. "Ouch! That hurt. What was that about?"

"*I'll give you my personal attention*. Geesh. I guess he's got it bad for you, Alona. I wish I was that lucky."

"He's trying to drum up business, that's all." But she now wanted to take Marshal Arts classes. "How about we both take a class?"

"Are you kidding?"

"No, I'm serious. After what's been happening in our neighborhood, I think it may be worth it." At least she could learn some new techniques to fight off criminals. Even though some of them deserved to die, it was too hard to cover up the deaths of thugs any more. Maybe, this is how she could finally settle down and not have to move again.

After Luke's visit, she caught Teresa glancing at her watch a couple times. She even did it herself and the time seemed to stop. "Okay, that's it. Today's been pretty dead. Let's close early," she said.

"Really? Are you docking me two hours for closing early?" Teresa asked.

"Do you ever clock in?"

"Uh, no."

"Then don't worry about it. You'll get the same pay as you always do. It's my call. Business is dead. I'll leave a note on the door." She quickly wrote a note about closing early and then her and Teresa did their closing routine. She counted out her drawer and put the money in the bank bag as usual. She wrote two checks, one for each of them. Then she stuffed the deposit into her purse.

It was ten minutes past four o'clock when the two of them left the store. Should she feel guilty? She was the owner, wasn't she? She would have time to stop by a store and buy some things for Matthias.

By the time she got to the grocery store, picked out the dog food, a leash, a couple bowls and a collar, it was close to five o'clock. The drive home was longer than usual because she was early, and the traffic was heavy. So much for saving time.

She just hoped Matthias' bladder held up all day. She was excited about her gifts for him. It was after 5:30 p.m. when she got home. When she unlocked her door, she thought she heard some shouting a few doors down. She knew most of her neighbors and that voice didn't sound familiar.

"Matthias? Where are you?" she called out. Something

blurred past her. *What in the world?* Matthias? She set everything down on the bar and went back out the door. *Was that him running past her?*

She glanced around her neighborhood from the front porch. She didn't see him anywhere. Instead, she heard an ambulance and a police car. She stepped out on the sidewalk about the time the police pulled into the area and parked in front of the Bensons' home. *Oh, no!*

The two officers ran to the house, knocking loudly. She held her breath until Mr. Benson opened the door. The two officers went inside. She didn't want to butt in, especially since she had been interviewed by the police twice today. She would wait until they left and make sure the Bensons were all right. She decided to continue her search for Matthias.

When she turned away from the Benson's side of the townhouses, she got a glimpse of Matthias.

"There you are! Come here, boy." He ran toward her. She knelt and hugged him. "Did you run past me? I bet you really had to relieve yourself, huh, boy? I got you some presents." She petted his head and then rubbed his chest. He licked her face and her neck. She stood and headed toward her home when she saw one police officer stand outside the Benson home. Then two familiar people showed up in a big, red truck. She stood on her sidewalk and watched the events unfold.

The male detective from earlier came over to her.

"Hello Ms. Gabriel. Nice to see you again. Is this your dog?" He reached over and petted Matthias.

"Well, I've adopted him recently," she said.

"What kind of dog is he?" the detective asked.

"I really don't know, but he likes me, so it doesn't really matter."

"You remember me, don't you? I'm detective Pete Cummings, and my partner, Elena Romero?"

"Oh, yes." She saw Elena come toward them.

"Hello," Elena said.

"The Bensons are my neighbors. I live in that townhouse," she said. She pointed to her unit.

"Did you see anything?" Elena asked her.

"No. I just heard the commotion outside and came to see what was going on," she said. She leaned over and petted Matthias. Maybe she should tell them she was really looking for her dog. She watched the two detectives exchange glances and then head over to the Benson's townhouse.

"Come on, Matthias. I'll fix you some dinner." She headed into her townhouse and closed the door. She opened the bag of dog food and set some in his new bowl. Then she got him some water in his other new bowl. "What do you think, boy?"

Matthias looked at the bowls and then at her and then at the bowls. He drank the water and then munched on some of the food. "I hope you like this food. I'm new at buying things for dogs."

She went back to the kitchen and heated up some leftovers for herself. After she ate, she put the new collar on Matthias and hooked a leash on it to make sure everything fit.

"You look good, boy." She petted his head and smiled. "I'm going back to the Bensons' and see if they need anything. They're an older couple and I'm afraid they won't ask for help, even if they do need it. You'll be all right, won't you, boy?"

He cocked his head one way and then the other. "You're so cute." She kissed his face and he licked her in the mouth.

"I'll be right back, Matthias, and when I return, we'll go

for a walk." She petted him one more time and headed to the Benson place.

The red truck was still nearby but the police car was gone. She knocked on the door.

Mr. Benson opened the door. "Mr. Benson, I came to see if there was anything I can do for you?"

"Come in, come in. Yes. Anna and I were fixing dinner when we were interrupted by a burglar."

"A burglar! Oh my gosh! Are you both all right?" She noticed the bruise by his eye.

"We're both a little shaken. Anna got the worst of it, I'm afraid."

"I would be glad to help you with your dinner, if you want?" she asked.

"Yes, please," Mrs. Benson called out.

Alona glanced over in her direction and saw Mrs. Benson sitting with her foot propped up with an ice pack on it. "Oh, my goodness!" She rushed over to where Mrs. Benson sat. "What can I do for you, Mrs. Benson?"

"My dinner is on the stove. I hope it's not ruined. I was just re-heating some leftovers tonight."

"Let me take care of that for you. I'll bring you both something to eat." She headed into the kitchen and found the food was on simmer. She quickly re-heated everything and served it on two separate dishes, one for each of them. Then she cleaned up the mess and headed home. The two detectives were still there when she left, and a few other people worked inside the Benson bedroom.

True to her word, she took Matthias for a walk around the neighborhood. It was about a mile around the loop. It was something she did for exercise every now and then.

"Well, Matthias, I need to figure a way for me to get you

outside while I'm at the shop because by the time I get home, you may not be able to hold it in."

She dressed for bed and found Matthias sitting at her feet, watching her. "Why do I get the feeling you aren't really a dog?"

Matthias sneezed. "God bless you!" she said. "If you're going to sleep with me, then you stay on that side and this side is mine." She climbed into bed. Before she turned out the light, Matthias was in the bed beside her, but under the covers.

She touched the side of his face. "Good night, Matthias."

She blinked twice when she thought she saw him wink at her.

3

———

Chapter Three

Alona Gabriel didn't seem to be as bad as he thought. It took him nearly two thousand years to finally locate her. The stories of the Nephilim being giants had been true, but not with this one. He knew she was part human, but all the others had been giants. So, what was her story? Why was she different? And what powers did she have? He crept closer to her, under the covers.

She was nice looking, that's for sure. She seemed in great shape, especially when he watched her dry her naked body after showering. It was all he could do to remain in dog form. She had him panting.

She genuinely cared for her neighbors and for lost dogs. This would take more time to investigate before he made his decision. And he was going to enjoy every minute of it. But today, he almost didn't get back in time. If she hadn't called out his name, he would still be downtown, in human form. Then how would that look? What would she think?

Alona awoke before her alarm. She felt something warm across her stomach. She glanced down and saw Matthias' paw on her belly and his muzzle was against her breast. Hmm. If she didn't know better, she would think Matthias was acting more human-like than dog-like.

"Good morning, Matthias. What did I tell you about sleeping on your side of the bed?" She turned toward him.

He raised his eyebrows, then covered his face with his paw.

"You know what you did. If you keep hogging the bed, you'll be sleeping in the living room." She rolled over and threw off her covers. Then she headed into the bathroom to start her daily routine.

After their morning walk, she started on her exercise routine. He sat in the doorway and watched her. When she finished, she made sure he was not in the bathroom this time. "I think you've seen enough of me naked, Matthias. You can wait here in the bedroom."

When they both finished breakfast, she walked him again. "I don't know if I should find someone to walk you while I'm gone, boy. I hate for you to be here all day and not be able to relieve yourself."

Once she was inside, she picked up her phone to check the time. "Oh my gosh! It's Saturday! I could've slept in today."

She remembered Teresa telling her she and her sister were going to the beach. "I need to get a life," she said. She glanced at Matthias. "Well, I guess you get to hang out with me today, Matthias. I don't have to work after all."

While she was up and dressed, she went ahead and did

the laundry. Then she made up her grocery list. "I'll buy you some toys today, Matthias. How about that?"

He barked. "I'll take that as a yes." Before she could grab her purse and head to the store, there was a knock at her door.

She peered out the peep hole and saw two men standing at her door. Matthias joined her and growled. "Yes?" she called out.

"Miami-Dade Police Department, Ms. Gabriel. We have a few questions to ask you."

She bit her fist. *Damn!* "Just a minute." She unlocked her door and opened it a few inches. "Yes?"

"May we come in?" They both showed her their badges.

She opened the door wider, and Matthias barked at them.

"Shhh! It's okay, boy." She showed them to her living room. "I was just about to go out when you knocked."

"This shouldn't take too long, Ms. Gabriel. I'm detective Davis and this is detective Jones." The two men sat on her sofa.

"How do you know my name?"

"The officers who interviewed everyone coming into the parking lot yesterday got everyone's tag numbers. We're investigating a crime that was committed the other day, downtown."

She sat across from them in a chair and Matthias sat at her feet. She tried to keep herself calm.

"What time did you leave your job, Ms. Gabriel," Davis asked her.

"I usually leave a few minutes after six. Maybe ten minutes later. I didn't look at the clock before I left, but that's about the time I usually leave."

"Did you have anyone with you when you left work?" Jones asked.

"I own a sandwich shop downtown and I have one employee. We both walk together each night to the parking garage unless one of us had to park somewhere else."

"Is your employee male or female?" Davis asked.

"Female."

"Did either of you encounter a man with a gun?" Davis asked her.

"No." Her heart pounded.

"Were you aware there was a camera in the parking lot?" Davis asked.

"No. Were you able to see who committed the crime?" she asked.

"We do have a clip of the incident," Jones said.

"Really? Then did you arrest the man with the gun?"

"No, Ms. Gabriel. He was found dead at the scene."

"Well, then the criminal got what he deserved, right?"

"Why do you say that?" Davis asked.

"Well, if the man was carrying a gun, then he was up to no good, right?"

"He became a victim when he was murdered." Jones said.

"How do you know it wasn't self-defense?" she asked.

Davis and Jones looked at each other and then back at her.

"What do you know, Ms. Gabriel?" Davis asked.

"All I know is what I saw on the tv. The man pointed a gun at someone. It looked like he was trying to rob them. Did you check his background to see if he had a record or something?" she asked.

"The news clip didn't show a man with a gun, Ms. Gabriel," Jones said.

"I thought I saw another clip that *did* show him holding a gun where they asked for people to call in if they knew anything."

Davis turned to Jones. "We'll check on that when we get back to the office."

"That's beside the point, Ms. Gabriel. When he was murdered, he became the victim," Jones said.

"I don't understand your logic. If the man pointed a gun at someone and threatened them, it could have been self-defense. I think you should leave it at that and be thankful you have one less criminal running the streets."

Jones looked at Davis and then back at her. "We've taken up enough of your time, Ms. Gabriel. If we need any more information, we'll be back." Davis stood and Jones joined him. She let them out the door. Before they left, she asked one final question.

"If someone pulled a gun on you, Mr. Jones, what would you do?" she asked. "If people can legally carry guns, can't they use them to defend themselves?"

"Do you have a permit, Ms. Gabriel?"

"No, I don't. And I don't own a gun."

"Thank you, Ms. Gabriel. We'll be in touch," Davis said.

She closed the door and watched them leave through the peep hole. Then she slid down to the floor and wrapped her arms around Matthias.

"I know you understand things, Matthias. They must have seen me kill that man. I did it in self-defense. He would have shot me or Teresa or both of us. He had an evil aura about him. He even smelled like he'd been around a demon. Teresa doesn't remember anything. I made sure of that." She had been petting him. She pulled him close and kissed his face. "I've been alone for so long, I don't know how to share my feelings anymore. You came into my life at just the right time, Matthias. But now, I'm afraid I'm going to need a lawyer." Matthias lay beside her and put his head in her lap.

"I tried real hard to avoid criminals." She continued to pet him. "I've moved so many times over the centuries. I've loved and lost so many good people. I just wanted to settle down, you know? I wanted to live a normal life for once." She wiped a tear streaming down her face. She sniffed and wiped at her nose. "I just can't stand by and watch a bully or criminal take advantage of anyone. Not when I can stop it. But all I've got going for me is the ability to grow tall and my strength."

Matthias stood up and licked her face. She kissed his muzzle. "I guess I better get to the store and get you some toys, huh?"

Matthias watched through the window as she drove off and then transformed into Luke. He didn't know how she was able to stop someone from killing her and her employee. But that demon scent? Could it be Raum, the demon he had been tracking all these years? Was Raum after her as well? A Nephilim would be a great asset to the demon world. From Alona's behavior so far, he felt she was a good person. Now he had to convince her to let him train her in ways to protect herself. If nothing else, she was just a lonely soul trying to help humanity the best she could.

Alona finished up her grocery shopping and chose some cool chew toys and some tennis balls to occupy Matthias' time. Now that she had someone to spend time with, she would take him to the dog park and maybe even the beach. She'd have to go early in the morning before people arrived, but that was okay with her.

When she pulled up into the parking lot, she thought she saw the curtain move. Was Matthias watching for her? She unlocked her door. "Matthias? I'm home," she said.

He came running from the bedroom and jumped up to look at what was on the table. "Look what I got for you, boy." She picked up the two chew toys and pulled off their packaging. "Here you go," she said. She put the first one into his mouth and Matthias ran off with it. "I hope you like it," she said.

She finished putting away her groceries, then opened the tennis balls. "Here, catch!" She tossed a ball toward him and he jumped up and caught it in his mouth. "Good catch! Would you like to go to the dog park?"

Matthias barked. "Okay, let's go." She grabbed her keys and his leash, fastening it onto his collar. Then the two of them went for a lengthy walk to the dog park.

There were lots of other people there with their dogs, so she kept Matthias on a leash. She tossed the tennis ball and he tried to retrieve it, but the leash was too short. She walked with Matthias a distance away and released him from the leash. Then she threw the ball, and he retrieved it. She noticed a man walking by himself, with no dog, out of the corner of her eye, to her right. By the time Matthias returned, there was a different man walking in front of her. Something felt wrong. Matthias growled as she struggled to put his leash back on. "You feel it, boy?" The man in front of her closed in. The man behind her, grabbed her face and covered her mouth. She bent forward, hard, grabbing his arm, and flipped him over her head.

"Hold him, Matthias!" she shouted. The man in front of

her, froze. "What do you want?" she shouted. The man raised his arms and then turned to run away. "Get him, Matthias!" Matthias ran and jumped the man, knocking him down. He barked and growled, baring his teeth, while standing on the man. She glanced around and when no one watched, she punched the man who had grabbed her, hard in the face, knocking him out. Then she dialed the police. A crowd gathered around the man Matthias stood on.

She dragged the unconscious man toward him and dumped him on top of the man Matthias held down.

"Yes, I want to report two men who attacked me today in the park." The people who had gathered backed up. She gave the police the address and stood watching the crowd. "These two men just attacked me. Did anyone else get attacked today?" she asked the crowd. No one responded. "Did anyone witness them attacking me?" A little girl raised her hand. "What did you see?" she asked her.

"I saw that man run toward you," she said. She pointed at the man on the ground. He struggled to get free, but the weight of the other man pinned him down. Plus, Matthias stood beside him, growling.

"Did you see anything else?" Alona asked.

"Yes. I saw that man grab your face." She pointed to the man on top.

"Thank you," Alona said. "Can you please tell that to the police when they arrive?"

The little girl nodded. Behind her stood a man and woman with a small dog on a leash.

Within minutes, a police unit arrived. They questioned the crowd of people and the little girl.

"I want to press charges, officer," Alona said.

"Do you know these men?"

"No. I've never seen them before."

"We'll need you to come down to the station to do that."

Just what she needed on her day off. "Sure."

Another unit arrived and hauled off the man she knocked out, while the first unit took the man on the ground.

"Well, Matthias, I guess we're going for a ride." She walked him back home to get her car. "See what I mean?" She turned to speak to Matthias. "Why can't I have a normal life, like everyone else?" After retrieving her purse, she loaded Mattias and herself into her car.

They drove to the downtown station and parked. Alona walked Matthias up the steps to the Police Department. Once inside, she headed for a desk in the main area.

"I need to press charges against two men who just attacked me in the park. The officers told me to come here and press charges."

"Here, fill this out. Do you have a lawyer?"

"No. Do I need one?"

"Yes. I would suggest you find a lawyer and have them work with you on this filing."

"Do you have any suggestions?"

"Well, I'm sure you can find something online."

"Uh, thanks. Come on, Matthias." She led him out the door and to the car. "Now what?" She glanced at Mattias. He cocked his head. "Let's go home, boy. I can think better at home."

By the time she got home, it was late afternoon. She researched online all the lawyers in the Miami area. She found a law office with several lawyers, but since it was Saturday, she would have to wait until Monday to make a call. She scribbled down the names and numbers. "The rest of the day is ours, Matthias. What would you like to do?"

Matthias walked over to the food bowl and dragged it around on the floor.

"Oh my goodness! You played hard today and helped capture a criminal. This calls for something special." She went into the kitchen and got him a treat. "I'm going to fix us some steaks. What do you think about that?"

Matthias barked. "I thought so." She got busy in the kitchen with seasoning the steaks. Then she fixed a salad for both of them. "I hope you like salad, Matthias."

He barked. "Good boy!" She petted his head. "Come on," she said. She led him out the back door to her small patio. She pulled the grill open and fired it up for the steaks. Then she went inside and got the potatoes going. "We're having mashed potatoes and gravy with our steak. How does that sound?"

Matthias spun around and barked. Once she got the potatoes under control, she put the steaks on the grill. She went back inside and grabbed a beer from the fridge and went out to watch the steaks.

"Hmm. It can't get much better than this, huh Matthias?" He stood between her legs while she sat sideways in a lounge chair. She petted his head. "If only you were the man of my dreams," she said. She pictured the good-looking man, Luke.

Matthias barked then jumped up with his feet on her thighs and licked her face. "I love you too, boy."

Soon after, the steaks were done. She took them inside and finished making the potatoes and gravy. She served the two of them at the coffee table. "This won't happen too often, boy, so enjoy it while you can."

When supper was finished, she took Matthias for a long walk. Then they sat on the couch and watched movies together.

Alona awoke to something wet on her face and realized Matthias was licking her. She glanced at the clock. It was almost eleven in the evening.

"I bet you need to go out, don't you, boy?"

Matthias barked. "Okay, let's go. She took him for a walk and when he did his thing, she brought him back inside.

"I think I'll get to bed as well, Matthias. I'm really tired. Today has been a long one."

She changed for bed while Matthias watched. Then she crawled into her bed and turned out the light. Within minutes, a cold, wet nose touched her back.

"Whoa!" She turned to face Matthias. "What did I tell you about hogging the bed?"

He moved his paw to touch her arm. "That's far enough, boy. You're acting a little too human in my opinion." She petted his head. "Thanks for helping me out today. You captured a criminal and saved me from harm. I owe you one."

He winked at her. *Yes, it was definitely a wink. There's something really different about this dog.* She turned away from him and closed her eyes. She needed rest. Everything else could wait until morning.

Matthias lay sleeping next to her. How could he tell her he was falling for her? If she could accept him as a dog, maybe she would like him as a human as well. He would have to convince her to join his martial arts class. Then, maybe, he could teach her how to defend herself. Today, while he was busy with the first criminal, he didn't see the second one attack her. But after hearing the little girl's account of what happened, he believed it. How did Alona knock the guy out?

She must be very strong to be able to drag his large body across the park and heave it onto the other man. It took three police officers to haul his large body into the police vehicle and she did it alone. He needed to know all her secrets. She had told him some of them earlier. And when she confessed she had loved and lost others in the past, it broke his heart. He wanted to comfort her as a man. He could only imagine how hard that was for her.

4
____

Chapter Four

After spending a nice weekend getting to know Matthias, Alona headed off to her shop. She felt better getting to share some of her feelings with him, knowing he could never tell anyone. But she felt he understood her pain. At least, he looked as if he did.

She made a stop at the bank and deposited the earnings from Friday, then continued to the shop. At some point during the morning, she would need to call a lawyer and make an appointment to go over the charges against the men who attacked her over the weekend. She might eventually need a lawyer for what happened in the garage, but she wouldn't mention that unless she was pressed.

She opened her shop. Then she got everything ready for the day, preparing the foods she would need for the sandwiches. She also had a delivery coming in sometime today. Before she knew it, Teresa came in.

"So, how was your weekend?" she asked Teresa.

"It was great! My sister and I met some cute guys and

then later we all went out for drinks and dancing." Teresa smiled during the telling of her adventure.

"Okay, so what's the guy's name?"

"What guy?"

"The one you're smiling about," she said.

"Oh, that guy. His name is Renaldo."

"And did the two of you make plans for another get-together?"

"Well, yes, we did." Teresa beamed.

"Good for you!"

"How about you? What did you do?"

"Let's say it was an interesting weekend."

"Come on. I want details," Teresa said.

"Did you give me all the details about Renaldo?"

"Okay, so we made out."

Alona glared at Teresa.

"Okay, so we had sex, too."

"Was it good?"

"Very."

"Okay, so I got to know Matthias more."

"Matthias? Who's he?"

"My dog. I thought I told you I found a dog last week."

"Oh, yeah. So, what did you do?"

"This dog is smart. It's like he's almost human. I was attacked in the dog park, and he helped me capture the two thugs."

"Oh, my gosh! You were attacked? That's awful."

"Yes. I need to call a lawyer today to make an appointment to charge the criminals." Alona glanced at her watch. "Let me do that while I'm thinking about it," she said.

She pulled out the small notepad with the phone number on it and punched in the numbers on her cell phone. The door chimed, so she stepped into the back office to finish her call.

When she came out, the good-looking martial arts guy was in her shop.

"Oh, hello!" she said. "This is early for you, isn't it?"

"Yes. I came to fetch you for a free lesson."

"What?"

"I didn't think you would be busy just yet, so I'm giving you a free lesson right now. Come on," he said. He reached over the counter and took her hand, gently pulling her out from around her counter.

"I can handle it while you're gone, Alona," Teresa said. "Uh, how long will she be gone?"

"I'll bring her back in an hour," Luke said.

"You do that, or I'll hunt you down," Teresa said. She chuckled and waved.

Alona pulled off her apron and tossed it back to Teresa. Luke grabbed her hand and walked out the door, holding her hand in his. His hand was large and warm. It felt strong and a little rough, like he'd worked hard all his life.

"I feel like I'm playing hooky from school," she said. He glanced at her and smiled. She realized his eyes were very familiar and brown. *Where had she seen such warm, brown eyes?*

They walked a few shops down on the right and he opened the door for her. Inside was a desk and a woman at the desk, dressed in a white, robe-like outfit. Behind the desk to the left was a small class of women dressed the same, with a male teacher. They were doing exercises of some sort.

Alona glanced down at what she was wearing. "I don't think I'm dressed right for this class."

"No, you aren't," Luke said. He still held her hand and

led her to the back where there was a smaller classroom, an office, and a set of bathrooms. "Go inside and you'll find an outfit you can wear. It's brand new." He leaned close to her ear. "You do look fantastic, though."

Caught off guard, she blinked several times. "Thank you." She closed the door behind her and changed into the white, robe-type outfit and removed her shoes.

When she came out, Luke took her by the hand to the smaller classroom. Now he was barefoot as well.

"You are now wearing a Gi," he said. "You'll be able to move better in this than your jeans and dressy blouse."

She stood before him, excited and a little nervous. He was just too good-looking to take her eyes off him, but she had to listen carefully. Her heart pounded as he took her other hand and faced her.

"I want you to be safe and learn to protect yourself, but first, I'll show you some exercises to get your body ready for the lessons."

"I exercise every day."

"I know you do."

"Uh, how do you know that?"

"I can tell by the firmness of your arms."

Her arms were hidden from him in this Gi. And before that, she wore a dressy blouse. She watched him pick up a couple of metal balls with a ring on each for a handle.

"Stand here with your feet apart and hold these out from your sides," he said.

She did as she was told. He moved close and raised her arms higher. "Now hold this position for five minutes," he said.

She rolled her eyes. These weights were so light, she could do this for way more than five minutes.

"Boring, huh?"

"Did I say that out loud?"

"No, but your eyes did. Instead of these warm-ups, I'll give you a list of exercises to do if you promise to do them every day."

"I promise."

"All right, then we'll jump right to the heart of the program," he said. He took the weights from her and set them off to the side. "Put your hands up like this." He demonstrated with his hands up near his face in a slightly fisted shape. "Now, stand like this." He stood beside her and had one foot forward and the other behind. "Keep most of your weight on the back foot."

She glanced up and noticed a large mirror on the wall, facing her. She could now see him from the front and the side.

"I'm going to show you the eight basic moves. Try to follow." Luke slid forward. She did the same. Then he slid back. She followed that. He slid to his left, so she slid left. Then he slid right, and she did the same. Then he moved forward in a diagonal, and she repeated that motion. Luke then moved forward in a left diagonal. Then he moved forward, driving his elbow up. After she repeated that, he did the same with the other elbow and she repeated that motion as well.

"Now, we do this again. See if you can remember the stances," he said.

Everything Luke did, she copied. She filed it away in her memory. This seemed easy enough so far.

"Now, I'm going to show you the basic punches," he said. "It mostly has to do with your hip rotation, so watch me carefully." He demonstrated a left jab, a jab cross, a hook, and an upper cut. She tried each one after he showed them to her.

"It seems easy enough," she said.

"It is. It's just knowing which one to use and when. Always keep your hands up to protect your face. Now I'll show you some kicks. This one you'll bring your knee up and out. It's good for blocking."

She tried it after Luke demonstrated it.

"Now this one is the roundhouse kick. You need to rotate your hips and use your shin to hit their femur." This time, he used her to demonstrate on. He didn't connect with her as in a real kick but stopped short when his foot touched her upper leg. "Now you try it," he said.

She tried the roundhouse. "What if the person is much smaller than me?" she asked.

"Then you will be hitting them in the side or the kidneys," he said. He took her hands and stood her before him. "I'm going to demonstrate some knee strikes. For this, just stand there and watch, then I'll let you try.

Luke demonstrated the forward thrusting strike after bringing the knee up and in. After that one, he showed her the round knee, swinging up and over. Then the last one was the offline knee, which was a diagonal strike. She repeated each one, just like he showed her.

"Wow, you did awesome for your first lesson," he said. He took her hand and walked her to the desk. His hand was warm and strong. She didn't want this time to end. "Now promise me you'll do these exercises." He handed her a sheet of paper with the exercises listed with pictures beside each one.

"I promise. And I keep my word."

He gazed into her eyes. "I believe you. Now, do you think you can remember these kicks and punches?"

"I...hope so. I will practice as much as I can remember. I had fun today."

"I'm glad you did. I want you to come back every day and work with me until you can do these without thinking about it."

"I'll try," she said.

"Do, there is no try," Luke said in a voice that sounded just like Yoda.

"That was cool. Do you do other voices as well?"

"If you have dinner with me, you can find out," he said.

"Well? Yes, I would love that." She smiled.

"Good. This Friday night okay with you?"

"It's very okay. How about seven?" Her heart pounded.

"It's a date." He ushered her to the bathroom so she could change back into her own clothes.

When she had changed, he walked her back to her shop. She hadn't been this close to a man in over a hundred years. He held her hand as they walked. A warm, tingling feeling ran through her veins. *Was she falling for this guy?* Well, she definitely wanted to continue this class.

When they got to her shop, she realized she hadn't paid him for his time. "I'm sorry. I forgot to ask you how much I owe you for the lesson?" she said. They stood before her door.

He leaned on her door with his elbow and gazed into her eyes. "I'll trade you Mui Thai lessons for one of those Italian sandwiches. But only if you personally make it for me," he said, touching her nose with his finger.

"Hmm, that sounds like a great deal to me. Come on." She wrapped her arm through his and walked inside, while Luke held the door for her.

Teresa had just finished with a customer when Alona walked behind the counter. She grabbed her apron and put it on, then washed her hands.

"How did the lesson go?" Teresa asked.

"Very good. Alona is a fast learner," Luke said.

"Thank you, Luke," she said. She pulled the items she needed for his sandwich and began putting it together.

"It's been pretty quiet so far," Teresa said. "I hope it picks up."

"It will," Luke said.

Alona handed him the sandwich and some chips and a drink. "Thank you for the sandwich, Alona," he said.

"You're very welcome. Thank you for the lesson."

"See you tomorrow, Alona."

"Bye," she said. She watched him walk out the door.

Teresa patted her shoulder. "I thought he had it bad for you, but I think you've got it worse."

"What's so bad about that?"

"Nothing. When was the last time you had a date?"

Alona thought back to the time she watched her last husband die of old age. So many people commented about how she hadn't aged, but he did. After his funeral, she moved away. It was too hard to explain to people who kept asking her what she took to not age. She had even dyed her hair gray so she would look older, but there were always the skeptics. She couldn't deal with those people, so she moved and started over. "It's been a while. I don't even remember." She wouldn't tell Teresa about her date with Luke. Not yet anyway.

"So, I take it you haven't had sex in a while, either?" Teresa asked.

"I'd rather not talk about it, okay?" Why bring up those memories?

A customer came in and then business picked up for the rest of the day. Alona and Teresa closed the shop at the usual time and headed to the parking garage.

"I just remembered I have an appointment tomorrow to see a lawyer," she said.

"A lawyer? What's up?" Teresa asked.

"I was attacked this past weekend, remember? I really need these classes Luke is teaching."

"Oh, my gosh, I totally forgot! I'm sorry that I teased you," she said.

"Tomorrow I'm going to open the shop, but I'll have to leave shortly after you arrive. I'll need you to cover for both of us because I don't know how long I'll be gone."

"Sure, no problem. What should I tell Luke?"

"If he asks, tell him I'll be there as quick as I can." She didn't want to miss seeing him after today. She walked Teresa to her car and then got into hers and drove home. She looked forward to seeing Matthias. At least now she had someone to confide in, even if he was a dog.

When she opened the door, Matthias jumped up to greet her.

"Hi, boy! I sure missed you today. Let me get your leash and we'll go for a walk." Moments later, she and Matthias had gone to the dog park. She let him take his time smelling all the benches and trees. She had forgotten to bring his toys. She would have to remember them the next time. She was anxious to share her day with him, but she waited until they were back home.

Once she had him fed and refilled his water bowl, she fixed herself a salad with leftovers. While she ate, she talked to Matthias. "I had a good day today, Matthias. How about you?"

He sat next to her while she sat at the table. He cocked his head.

"I met this really hot guy in my shop the other day. But today, he came back and got me for some martial arts lessons. I had fun. He gave me homework, so once my food is digested, I have to do my new exercises. I don't think I'll have time in the morning." She finished her meal and cleaned the kitchen. Then she settled on the couch to watch a movie with Matthias.

"You know, I hope Luke and I keep doing those lessons because I really enjoyed his company. He even asked me out for a date. Can you believe it?"

Matthias barked. "Yes?" He barked again. She put her arm around Matthias. "It's been so long since I've had a man in my life, Matthias. People like Luke just don't come along very often." Matthias licked her face. "Awe." She kissed his face. "You are so easy to love, Matthias, but I hope Luke is a better kisser than you." Matthias barked again.

When the movie ended, Alona went into her workout room and glanced at the exercises Luke had for her. Since she didn't have the weights he used, she improvised with a couple bags of canned foods in each hand. Most of the exercises appeared to be isometric exercises, something she hadn't done in a while. She worked her way down the paper and made notes to buy some weights and a belt to use for stretches. Most of the exercises seemed easy. She only did one set of each for her first time. She would do these again tomorrow, but maybe work up to two sets or use heavier weights. When she finished, she noticed Matthias had been watching her from the doorway.

"Well, I did what I promised, boy. You are my witness. These exercises just seemed too easy tonight." She glanced at her watch. "You need to go outside for a walk, don't you?"

Matthias sat up and barked. "Okay, let's go."

She walked him around the neighborhood, then found herself walking toward the dog park again. She kept to the lighted places and then headed home.

After locking up, she took a quick shower and got ready for bed. Matthias had already crawled under the covers before she could get under them herself.

"I forgot to tell you something Matthias," she said. She propped herself up and glanced at him. His head was on the pillow and he raised it when she spoke.

"I have an appointment with a lawyer tomorrow morning. It concerns those two thugs you helped me with. I sure hope I get done in time to see Luke and to take his class."

Matthias raised his brows, then lay back on the pillow. She lay on her side watching Matthias after turning off the light. He looked like a dog, smelled like a dog, and most of the time, he acted like a dog. But why did she feel he wasn't really a dog? Was she reading too much into his behavior? Or was she so lonely, she was inventing something that wasn't there?

She closed her eyes and thought of Luke, with his warm, brown eyes, his blondish brown hair, and that smile. She just about melted the first time he smiled at her. Her eyes opened. There was Matthias, with his eyes closed, facing her. He had the same, unusual hair coloring as Luke. His eyes were warm and brown as well. Then, as if he knew she was looking at him, he opened his eyes. She blinked twice when he opened his mouth into a smile.

5

____

Chapter Five

The next morning, when Alona awoke, she found a paw across her stomach. She rolled over to face Matthias.

"What have I told you about being on your side of the bed?"

Matthias opened his eyes and licked her arm. She threw off the covers and stretched. Today, she felt a little sore. Maybe it was the workout she had yesterday and the new exercises. She didn't think they did anything for her, but she definitely felt something. She rotated her arms. Yes, they were a little stiff.

"Well, Matthias, I feel those exercises today." She quickly got dressed so she could walk Matthias and get her workout routine in before heading to the shop.

Before she drove downtown, she made sure she had the police report she was to fill out. The lawyers weren't too far from where she had her shop, so she hoped it wouldn't take too long. She got to the building about her usual time. The police tape was still up in the section where the body had been found, but there weren't any police officers around. She parked her car and headed to the shop. By the time she had everything prepped, Teresa came in. She headed out the door and back to the parking garage. Her appointment was with someone named Del Torro. She found the office and went inside.

"Hello, Ms. Gabriel, I'm Juan Del Torro. How can I help you?"

"I was told to fill this form out by someone at the police department if I want to press charges. I want to press charges."

"Okay. How about we start at the beginning," Del Torro said.

She explained what had happened on that Saturday and showed Mr. Del Torro the police report. He looked it over.

"So, you have a witness. That's good."

"Yes, but she's a minor. Her parents did sign the report, though."

"Well, that's still good. I'll be glad to take the case. I can file this week." He went over the fees, and she wrote him a check for the initial payment. If she won the case, the criminals would pay the court costs and her expenses, plus any damages.

"You know, I don't care about the money. I just want these thugs off the street for a long time. No one should feel unsafe or endangered in a dog park or any park for that matter."

"I agree. I will keep you posted on the events and the court date," he said. She gave him her information and then headed back to her shop. She glanced at her watch. It was a little after ten. That was the time Luke came for her yesterday.

She was excited to see Luke again and stopped by his shop on her way to her own shop.

"Hi, I hope I didn't miss you this morning," she said.

"No. I was just about to go get you."

"I had an appointment with a lawyer this morning."

"Oh?"

"Yes, I was attacked last weekend and my dog helped save me. I'm pressing charges against the criminals who attacked me."

"This is exactly why you need me," he said. He took her hand and led her to the bathroom. "Get changed so we can get started."

She hurriedly dressed, while his words ran through her mind. *This is why you need me.* Not, this is why you need my classes. *Interesting choice of words.*

Once they were together in his small classroom, he reviewed the different stances. She remembered them and was able to do them with him and not after him.

"Very good."

"I'm a little sore from the exercises."

"So, you kept your promise."

"I told you I would."

"Yes, you did."

Then he reviewed the punches. She caught on to those as well. Then Luke had her practice the punches while he blocked them. "Pay attention to what I'm doing so when I throw those punches, you can block them as well."

Then, true to his word, Luke threw the punches at her, and she tried to remember how he blocked them. Luke stopped several times to show her how to do the blocks.

"I know I didn't show you the blocks, but you're catching on quite well."

She smiled at the compliment. She couldn't remember the last time she was given a compliment, so it felt good.

Then Luke went over the kicks, and she kept up with him.

"Now, I'm going to block those kicks, so you keep practicing them. If you lose your balance, I got you."

She did the kicks like he showed her, but the blocks were new. He grabbed her leg a time or two and she hopped and grabbed his shoulder, thinking she was about to fall.

"I got you. I won't let you fall," he said.

"Promise?" She tried the roundhouse kick, and he caught her leg. They were very close.

"Promise." He touched her forehead with his. His gaze was intense.

She touched the side of his face. "Your eyes remind me of someone," she said.

He lowered her leg. "Really?"

She nodded.

"I hope it's not a current boyfriend."

"No, it's my...uh, never mind."

Then he smiled that smile.

"Is it hot in here?"

"No." He felt her forehead. "You don't have a fever. Are you feeling okay?"

"Yes. I'm good."

"Okay, let's do a few punches and kicks together." He showed her how to combine the two. She followed what he demonstrated. "Now, I'll let you continue those while I block you."

They did the combination several times, but the last one caught her off guard and she almost fell, but Luke caught her in his arms. She instinctively wrapped her arms around his neck, and he pulled her close into a hug. A very nice, long hug. Her heart pounded at his nearness. She felt something move against her stomach. She now knew he felt something for her by his physical reaction, just like she felt for him, but she didn't want to let go. His arms tightened around her, so she tightened her arms around him.

He whispered in her ear. "I think we need to stop for today." He loosened his grip.

She reluctantly loosened her grip. His words came back to her. *This is why you need me. Yes, it is.*

He waited for her to change and then held her hand while walking her back to the shop. There was that awkward silence as they walked past the few doors.

"Uh, did you want me to fix your favorite sandwich today?" she gave him a sideways glance.

"I would love that." He stopped to gaze into her eyes.

"And I would love to continue our training."

"Me, too." He opened the door for her.

She felt the awkwardness fade away as her heart raced. She busied herself behind the counter fixing his sandwich. Teresa asked what he wanted to drink and what chips he liked. By the time Alona finished making his sandwich, she felt back to normal.

"See you tomorrow, Alona. Don't forget your exercises."

"I promised, remember?"

"Yes, you did."

She watched him walk out the door.

"Well, you seem pretty happy today."

"I am very happy. I talked to the lawyer this morning and then had my lesson. Luke said I'm catching on pretty good."

"Good for you!"

After a while, business picked up. They had a line almost to the door. When the line dwindled down to a couple people, someone called out her name.

"Oh, hello, Ms. Romero," she said. It was the detective she had met when the burglaries occurred.

"It's Cummings, now."

"Cummings? Wasn't that your partner's name?" Alona asked.

"Yes, and now we're married."

"Congratulations! What will you have today?"

"I'll take a tuna sandwich on the wheat bread with chips and a water."

"Coming right up," Teresa said.

"Is Detective Cummings joining you?" Alona asked.

"Unfortunately, no. The captain assigned him to the Vice Squad."

"Why?"

"Because they don't want married couples working together."

"That's too bad. I...uh, never mind. I think if a married couple works well together, they shouldn't be separated."

"I totally agree with that," Elena said. She paid for her sandwich and Teresa brought it to her, along with her water and chips.

"Thank you. I think I'll eat in here, if you don't mind."

"Go right ahead," Alona said. She watched Detective Cummings sit at one of the tables. Her conversation reminded her of the times she and her past husbands had worked together. Back in the day, people could do that without question. Maybe it was different with law enforcement.

The last customer left, so Alona wiped down her counters. Then she went out to wipe off the empty tables. The detective was finishing up her sandwich.

"I plan to visit the Bensons after this to make sure everything is okay with them," Detective Cummings said.

"Oh, I think they will enjoy the company," Alona said.

"Good. Well, thank you for a great sandwich, ladies."

"You're welcome. Come back any time."

Alona watched Detective Cummings leave. "Well, she found her happily ever after."

"How can you say that? She said her captain separated them," Teresa said.

"Deep down, she was happy. I could sense it. The captain is a temporary problem."

It was late afternoon and business slowed down a lot. Alona had everything cleaned and ready to close before the last customer left.

"So, tell me about this Renaldo guy you are going out with," she said.

"He's tall with black hair. His eyes are brown, and he's got the cutest dimple on his chin."

"What? No pictures?"

"Oh, I have pictures."

Alona locked up and the two headed out the door to the parking garage. Teresa showed her the selfies she took when they were on the beach.

"So, how many times have you two gone out?"

"Well, the beach doesn't count since we met there. But we went out the next night to some dance clubs. Then I saw him last night, so twice."

"Wow, that's a record for you, isn't it?"

"Yes, I guess it is. We have a date this weekend as well."

"Good for you. Maybe you'll get your happily ever after, too."

~

Alona drove home thinking of how many happily ever afters she's had. Did she deserve another one? Probably not. But did she want one? Yes, yes, she did.

Matthias greeted her at the door, wagging his tail. He didn't jump up, but he acted as if he was glad to see her. Once she put her stuff down, she grabbed a toy and the leash and the two of them went for a walk. She took him to the dog park and tossed the tennis ball for him. He caught it every time. His reflexes were fast. "I'm impressed, Matthias. You are so good." He spun around and sat beside her. "I forgot your treats, Matthias. Can you forgive me? I promise I'll give you some treats when we get home, okay?"

Matthias barked.

"I take that as a yes. Okay, boy, let's go get that treat."

Matthias ran home. She realized she was getting more exercise from the run, so she let him run as fast as he wanted, but she was able to keep up. That was one of her gifts. She could go as fast as any animal, even faster if the distance was shorter. Once inside, she kept her word and gave him a couple dog biscuits. She refilled his water bowl and then gave him some food. She had nothing left over, so she prepared a meal that would last a couple days. While the chicken baked in the oven, she worked on her new exercises. She had to improvise again since she didn't stop to buy the weights. She finished cooking her meal, then sat down to eat it.

"How was your day, Matthias?" She didn't expect an answer, but she wanted to tell him about Luke. "I had another lesson with Luke today. He taught me some new moves for blocking. But one move almost knocked me off my feet. He caught me, though. We shared a nice, long hug." She glanced at Matthias, who seemed to be really listening. He sat with his head cocked. "I like him, Matthias. I like him a lot. We have a date this Friday night. I can't wait for you to meet him.

I almost lost it today. When I held her in my arms, I lost all logical thought. I didn't want to let go. I let human feelings take over. Had my desires for her done this? These human feelings are strange, but pleasant.

She hugged me back as if she wanted to hang on, like maybe she didn't want me to let her go. But that's not part of my mission. Finding out if she had a good heart and was in service to God, was my mission. And stopping the demon who searched for her.

When she took me in as Matthias, she heard my thoughts. She could hear me clearly say my name. I will speak to her through Matthias. But now, she wants me to meet Luke. Maybe she will open her thoughts to Matthias and I will eventually be able to reach her telepathically as Luke.

Matthias lay on his side of the bed, facing the wall, his head resting on Alona's spare pillow. The pillow once smelled of her, but now it was taking on his own scent. He felt something heavy across his chest. He glanced down and saw her arm. She had finally reached out to him. He rolled over to face her. She still slept with her arm around him. Should he try changing back to Luke so he could feel his arms around her? He wanted to but it would startle her. He didn't want to anger her but letting this Matthias thing go on for so long would do just that.

He would have to tell her the truth. This temptation to hold her and kiss her grew more intense the longer he was around her. If he told her the truth, would he lose her forever?

The next morning, Alona rushed through her routines so she could see Luke. She had thought of him during the night, and she hadn't let thoughts of men cloud her thinking before. When she awoke, she was surprised to see her own arm around Matthias. He didn't seem to mind and even licked her 'good morning.'

She made sure Matthias was taken care of before she left. She thought maybe he spoke to her before she left for work. It was a soft, *'Be careful,'* kind of warning. Or did she imagine that? When he licked her face 'goodbye,' she heard the warning.

In any case, it wouldn't hurt to be more careful. She stopped by the bank to make her deposit and headed on to the shop.

Once she had everything prepped for the day, Teresa came in to work. When everything was set, she turned on the open sign and stepped out on the sidewalk to greet the morning. Before she turned to go back inside, she saw Luke heading toward her.

"Good morning!" she said.

"It is now." He smiled.

There it was. That smile. It was a combination happy and sexy if there were such a thing. She wanted to keep watching him, so she stood outside while he walked toward her. Even his walk seemed to exude confidence.

"What brings you here so early?" she asked.

He leaned close and whispered. "The thought of seeing you."

Her eyes widened. *Did he feel for her the way she felt for him?* She heard a faint 'yes.'

She wrapped her arm through his. "Come in."

"I'd rather take you with me," he whispered.

Her heart pounded. She opened the door and stuck her head inside. "Teresa? I'll be back shortly!" Then she went with Luke to his shop.

She had changed into the Gi and faced Luke on the mat.

"I'm going to perform the punches and kicks I've taught you and I want you to block them," he said.

She stood ready. She forced her memory to bring back the counter moves he showed her the day before. Things came back to her as they went along.

"Good! You're doing really good!"

She stumbled a time or two, but Luke caught her. "I've got you!" he reminded her. The time seemed to fly by.

When it ended, he walked her to the bathroom where she changed. Before she headed out, she leaned on the door. *I wish this time with Luke was much longer.* Then she heard a faint '*me, too.*' She straightened. '*Is that you, Luke?*'

'*Yes.*'

She pulled the door open. Luke stood on the other side. "Did you just speak to me telepathically?"

'*Yes.*' His gaze was intense. Then he smiled a sexy, 'I'm up to something' kind of smile.

"How long have you had that gift?" she asked.

'*A very long time. Try it. You might like it.*'

She moved close to him and poked him in the chest. "Do or do not. There is no try."

He smiled and wrapped his arms around her and hugged her. He inhaled her scent. She did the same. As her arms tightened, so did his. And then his erection brought her back to reality, but she didn't let up on the hugging.

'I would like to help you with this problem,' she said telepathically.

'And I want you to help me, but not today.'

"Are you walking me back to my shop?"

"Yes. I'm looking forward to your sandwich."

She didn't care that Teresa saw the two of them holding hands. And she didn't care that Teresa knew something was going on. She was in a great mood, and she wanted to share it.

Before she gave Luke his sandwich, Detective Cummings came into the shop. "Hello Detective Cummings," Alona said.

"Oh, you remembered me."

"How can I forget? I try to remember all my customers. What will you have today?"

"I'll try the ham and Swiss wrap with water and chips." Alona gave the order to Teresa. Then she introduced Luke to her. "This is Luke, our neighborhood martial arts instructor."

"Oh, nice to meet you. I'm checking into renting the shop next to yours for an investigation I'm doing."

"Oh? What are you investigating, exactly?" Luke asked.

"I'm investigating a security company that left business cards at each of three businesses that were recently robbed."

Alona thought of the demon who had tried to leave his card with her. *Should she mention it?*

Luke glanced at her, then at Detective Cummings. "That is unusual," he said.

"You know, I may need to check your facilities as well as the empty shop," Detective Cummings said.

"Why is that?" Luke asked.

"Well, this company doesn't want anyone present while they install their equipment. I find that very odd, and I'm stubborn enough to want to see what's the big deal."

"I don't blame you. Are you thinking they may have something to do with the robberies themselves?" Luke asked.

6

———

Chapter Six

"**Y**es! It's like you read my thoughts." *'Just like Pete does.'*

'And who is Pete?'

Elena Cummings glanced at Luke. "Did you just say something?"

"No." *'But I did speak to you telepathically.'* Luke said.

"Here's your wrap," Teresa said. She handed it to the detective.

"Thank you." Elena took her food and sat at a table.

Luke noticed Detective Cummings glancing back at him. Then he heard her say, *'Pete is my husband, a detective, and a former angel.'*

'I thought so. Come and see me after your visit with the realtor.' Luke reached out and touched Alona's hand. "Thank you for the sandwich, Alona."

She smiled at him. "My pleasure."

He left the shop and sent *'I'm looking forward to seeing you again,'* to the detective.

Luke distinctly heard Alona's thoughts about the demon. She had seen him, but she didn't mention this to the detective, or to him. But Alona was just beginning to open up to him. He didn't want her to close off her mind to him. Not now. But if Alona had seen the demon, then Raum knew who Alona was and where she worked. Luke would definitely need some allies to help him protect Alona. She was vulnerable.

After about thirty minutes, the detective came in to the Martial Arts Academy. When Luke felt her presence, he stood before her.

"Come to my office," he said. He reached out a hand to help her off the sofa.

"Wow, I was sunk into the seat," she said.

"It happens to everyone. It's temporary seating anyway." He didn't know how long this mission would last, so he didn't worry about the furniture.

He ushered her to a seat in his small office/studio. It was big enough for one-on-one teaching. "Now we can talk."

"How is it you are telepathic?" she asked.

He had met both her and Pete at Alona's townhouse complex when he was Matthias. "If Pete was a former angel, didn't he tell you about me?"

"What do you mean?"

"I thought he would have mentioned I am an angel as well."

"Wait, he told me Alona's dog was an angel," she said.

He stood up and leaned on the desk and transformed into Matthias.

She stood up. "Well, in that case, he was right," she said.

He transformed back into Luke.

"So, does Alona know?"

"No, not yet. And I want to keep it that way for now." He had to find the right way and time to tell her.

"Why are you telling me this?" she asked.

"Because I need an ally and so do you."

"How can I help you?"

"Alona is being tracked by a demon, but she doesn't know that. I can only watch out for her when I'm physically present. My presence in this studio is only temporary, so I can be near her during the day."

"How can I possibly help you?"

"You can be my eyes and ears here, while I search for the demon."

"My captain won't allow me to lease the shop next door, otherwise, I could help you."

"I will work something out for you. This demon must be stopped, and only by an angel. What you want to do will give you the information you need to pursue your investigation."

"Okay, what's the first step?"

"Tell the realtor you'll take the shop. I will work on your captain. There are things I can do in the day if you are watching out for Alona. You know she is a Nephilim, right?"

"Uh, well, Pete mentioned that she might be. What exactly is that?"

"She's half angel and half human. I'm trying to teach her how to use her humanness to protect herself and others, rather than her Nephilim self. She's very strong and can sense a demon, but the way she responds will get her arrested and exposed."

"Okay, I'll speak to the realtor about the shop."

"Remember, this is our secret. Alona must not know. Not yet."

"I will tell Pete, of course."

"He is the only one you can tell, but no one else."

"All right, and you will continue to keep me informed?"

"Yes, we will speak telepathically from here on out."

After Detective Cummings left, Luke intervened with the captain and his superiors. He couldn't interfere with free will, but he could influence them in their decisions, especially if they didn't know all the details. He could at least show them more of the big picture.

A sense of foreboding came over him. Something was about to happen, but he couldn't get a handle on it. He sent a message to Alona. *'Be careful.'* He did some meditation to see what was in store, but he was interrupted by the receptionist.

"Someone is here to see you."

Detective Cummings walked into the office. "Luke, you would save me a lot of time if I could get you to oversee the installation of the security system. I need to know what they are hiding when they install it."

"Make the appointment and I'll be there. Just let me know the time and place."

"Thanks."

Alona and Teresa headed to the parking lot after a long day. She looked forward to seeing Matthias and telling him about Luke.

Teresa made a comment about her date with Luke.

"Give you the details? I don't think so. Do you tell me the details of your dates?" Alona asked.

"Oh, hello," Detective Cummings said.

"What are you doing here?" Alona asked.

"Well, I guess we will be downtown neighbors for a while," she said.

"How is that?"

"I was able to lease the shop next door to the Martial Arts Academy."

"Oh? That's where Luke works," Alona said. Suddenly she felt danger surround her.

"Hold it right there, ladies," a male voice said.

'Great! Too many witnesses to do anything.' Something covered her head. Her arms were pulled back behind her. Something tight restrained her arm movements. Should she go along with this? She could react at any time, but timing was everything. And now she had two others to protect besides herself. She heard some shuffling and she was shoved around.

Screeching tires came toward them. Finally, the sound stopped, and she was forced inside a vehicle. It felt like a van. The two other women were shoved against her. Their voices were muffled.

"Sorry," someone said.

She went over the kicks and punches Luke had taught her, but they wouldn't do her any good right now. Before now would have been a good time to use them. Why didn't she think of that? She had been distracted. She hadn't even felt the presence of danger until it was too late.

The van turned abruptly, and her head hit the side of the seat. "Ouch!"

"Alona, is that you?" It sounded like Teresa.

"I'm here, too," Detective Cummings said.

Another sharp turn and all three of them rolled into each other.

"Sorry," Detective Cummings said.

The vehicle stopped abruptly. The doors opened. Someone pulled her arm, yanking her out of the vehicle. When her hood was yanked off, it took a few moments for her eyes to adjust to the light. She stood beside Detective Cummings and Teresa. Standing in front of them were three tall people. They appeared to be men wearing ski masks.

"He wants this one," One of the men grabbed her arm. He pulled her with him to an office. She glanced around quickly and realized she was in a warehouse of some sort. He opened the door and shoved her inside.

The demon was there. She could smell him before she made eye contact. A man sat at the desk, the demon beside him, and one other man, besides the escort. The man who brought her to the office yelled at her and told her to sit down, shoving her into the seat. She lost her balance on the straight-back wooden chair from his force. She managed to regain her composure, when the demon stood before her. His foul stench was strong.

"You know why you are here, Noura Hashim?"

Her eyes widened. She hadn't told anyone her real name, but she wouldn't admit anything to this demon.

"I want you to work for me," he said.

"I work for a higher God, so drop dead. Oh, wait, you already are, that's why you stink."

He slapped her so hard she lost her balance again, almost falling off the chair. Now she was mad. She could easily take these men, but the demon was a different story.

She pulled at her restraints and grunted from the force, breaking the plastic tie in two. Then she stood, grabbing her own chair. She swung at the demon, but he disappeared. The man who brought her into the room took a swing at her with a large bat. She used her super speed to dodge the bat.

Since she still had the chair in her hands, she connected it with the man sitting at the desk. The chair shattered.

The man with the bat swung at her shoulder but she was faster and rushed across the room, grabbing another chair.

The third man in the room pulled out a gun. It was the detective's gun. She connected the chair with the man's head, and he dropped the gun. Another chair shattered.

The man with the bat came at her again. This time, she lifted the desk to protect herself from his swing. He managed to crack the desk. She took half the desk and threw it at him, finally putting him down. Her heart pounded. She had to get out of here. When she reached for the door, it opened, and another man rushed in. She grabbed him and tossed him through the window. Well, half of him went through. The other half was still inside the office. She reached for the detective's gun, tucking it into her jeans, and ran to the door. Before she could leave, another man came in. This one had a gun as well. She grew as tall as the room and grabbed him by the throat, breaking his neck. She tossed him over her shoulder. She continued to the door when another man came inside. Her shoulders sagged. *Are you kidding me? How many men are there?*

She was close enough to this one, she drove her elbow into his face like Luke had showed her. He dropped at her feet. She turned and grabbed the other half of the desk and dropped it on him and he collapsed.

She ran out the door to freedom and saw the detective and Teresa running toward the parking lot.

"How did you escape?" the detective asked.

"Hold still," she said. She grabbed the detective's restraints and broke them in two. "Here." She handed the detective her gun. Then she rushed to Teresa and broke her restraints as well. "Let's get out of here," she said.

"Is someone going to tell me what's happening?" Teresa asked.

"I escaped, that's all you need to know," she said. *If they knew what she had done, they would be terrified of her.* Before they got very far in the parking lot, a large red truck pulled up in front of them.

"Pete! It's Pete!" the detective shouted. But there was someone with him.

"Luke?" *What was he doing here?*

Both men got out of the truck and ran toward them.

"How did you know we were here?" Alona asked Luke.

She watched the two detectives embrace. "We need to call this in," the woman detective said.

"No! We need to leave this place. Now!" she said. Her heart still pounded. She didn't want to be here anymore. She couldn't get caught. She couldn't.

"Alona, they need to do their job," Luke said. He put his arm around her. "Tell me what happened. Please, Alona. Tell me."

His touch was somewhat comforting, but the need to leave was overwhelming. She tried to compose herself. She wiped her face and realized she was drenched in perspiration.

Luke turned her to face him and hugged her. He held her tight. She could feel waves of comfort flowing over her. Was that her imagination, or was he just what she needed? She reached out and hugged him back. She didn't want to let go, and she didn't want to re-live those terrifying moments. She felt his lips against her forehead. She liked that.

She glanced up at him. "We were kidnapped. I was taken

into a room and shoved around. One man slapped me hard and I lost it. I tore off my restraints and I beat the crap out of all of them."

"Did you even try the moves I showed you?" Luke asked.

"I did on the last one. I finished him off with a piece of furniture, though."

He lifted her chin and gazed into her eyes. "We'll work on that, but are you okay?"

"Yes, I'm just angry right now."

Luke held her a few more minutes in a tight hug. Her shivering had slowed significantly after he sent calming waves of energy through her. She continued to hug him back. He sent her a message telepathically, *'this is why you need me.'* He hoped it would help her to feel comfortable around him.

He felt her bury her head in his neck. She took deep breaths to calm down even more. He stroked her back to help the calming energy flow.

He glanced around while holding Alona and saw Pete and Elena comforting Teresa. They were all using the deep breathing to calm down.

"We'll take you girls back to the parking garage when we finish here," Pete said.

"What are we waiting for?" Teresa asked.

A police cruiser pulled into the parking lot and stopped beside them.

"They will have questions for all of us before we can leave," Pete said.

"I've got to get home to my dog," Alona said.

"Trust me, Alona, he will be fine," Luke said.

Another cruiser pulled into the parking lot. The two units separated everyone and started the questioning, one at a time.

A third unit pulled up and the officers went into the warehouse. Within minutes, a couple ambulances pulled into the warehouse. He noticed several body bags coming out on gurneys and loaded into the ambulances. Luke had a feeling that Alona left out a few details. He hoped she would confide in Matthias.

When he and Alona were together, he held her hand. He wanted to give her strength to get through this. He put his arm around Teresa to help calm her down and she finally seemed like she was back to normal.

There were several minutes where Pete and Elena went into the warehouse with the police. Overall, the ordeal took about an hour on their part. The police, EMTs and detectives were there after everyone loaded into Pete's truck. Luke sat between Alona and Teresa and rode to the parking garage.

Pete made sure Elena and Teresa were safely in their cars before he left. Luke walked Alona to her car. He moved her hair away from her face and tucked it behind her ear.

"I wish you would open up to me, Alona," he said.

"What do you mean?"

"I think you're hiding something. I want to get to know you better, but I can't if you can't be honest with me." But he had to be honest with her as well. He had to tell her the truth, so she would know why he was here in the first place. But if he did tell her, would she still want to be with him? *Who was he kidding?* He couldn't protect her if he was no longer an angel. He didn't want to risk that.

Alona's eyes widened. "I am being honest with you. There are some things about me that I've never shared with anyone before. I just don't know if you're ready to hear about it. I don't want to lose you. And if I told you everything, you wouldn't want to know me anymore."

"I don't frighten easily, Alona. I promise you, whatever you've done in your past would not change the way I feel about you now." He couldn't take this relationship any further, though. "I hope you'll continue to work with me. Will I still see you tomorrow?"

"Of course. You can't get rid of me that easily," she said. "Besides, we still have a date on Friday, don't we?"

"Yes, yes we do."

Alona got into her car and drove off.

How was he going to pull off a date? He had no vehicle and no place to live except at her house as a dog.

When Alona got home, she greeted Matthias and he seemed excited to see her. She had a lot to tell him, but she would wait until after their walk.

Once they were inside and settled with dinner, she started filling him in. "I hope you don't mind me telling you about my day, Matthias. I mean, you can't say no, right?"

Matthias barked.

"Okay, then." She started with the abduction and then the fight in the warehouse office. She even mentioned the demon. Then she thought about what Luke said. "I don't know why I can talk to you and not Luke. I'm afraid I'll lose him, Matthias. I don't want to lose him."

Matthias put his paw on her thigh. She glanced at him.

"You think I should tell him everything?"

Matthias barked.

"Okay. I will. Maybe on our date."

Matthias jumped up and licked her face.

Later that night, when she got herself ready for bed, she thought about Luke again. She even let Matthias snuggle next to her in the bed.

"For some reason, Matthias, you remind me of Luke, and he reminds me of you. Why is that?"

Matthias raised his brows.

"No offense, boy, but sometimes, I wish you were Luke."

7

———

Chapter Seven

Matthias' heart raced hearing Alona's words, but he couldn't show any signs that he knew about her confession as Luke. He only had a couple days before the date. He would confess the truth to her then as well. He couldn't imagine doing that in a public place, though.

He could manifest a car and drive her to a movie, but somehow, he needed to talk to her in private. The only place he felt comfortable was in her home. If she was uncomfortable with the truth, she could lose both him and his shape shifting self.

He thought of the past life she confided in him. She didn't need another painful memory. Should he tell her the truth? Or just walk away? But if he didn't tell her, there were two others who could tell her the truth. In either case, he hoped she could forgive him.

If it hadn't been for the warmth of Alona's arm over his

body, his sleep would have been fitful. He enjoyed her touch.

Alona got her routine in and dressed as usual for the day when she got a call from the lawyer. Mr. Del Toro had filed the papers with the court and would let her know when he had a court date as soon as he found out. She put it out of her mind and drove to the shop. She looked forward to seeing Luke again.

Once her shop was opened, a couple detectives from North Miami came in to ask her some questions about the latest incident. The questions were the same as before, so she had nothing new to tell them. One of them leaned on her counter. "If I were you," he began, "I would get a lawyer."

"Am I being charged with anything?" she asked.

"Not today," the other one said. They walked out her door after that.

"What are you going to do now?" Teresa asked.

"I have a lawyer who is bringing charges against the two men who attacked me in the park. I could ask him," she said.

Although they didn't say it, the two detectives had implied she was a suspect in a murder case. When did self-defense become murder against criminals? What happened to justice?

"I saw the news last night," Teresa said.

"Oh, yeah? I didn't even turn on the tv. Instead, I had a long conversation with Matthias."

"Who is Matthias?" Teresa asked.

"My dog, remember?"

"Your dog carried on a conversation with you?"

"Well, sort of."

Teresa shook her head. "The newscaster said that five bodies were recovered in that office. What happened, Alona?"

"They were all bullies, Teresa, but they meant to hurt me. And I don't think you and Elena would have left that place alive if I hadn't stopped them."

"What do you mean?"

"Do you remember that demon that came in here?"

"The good-looking one?"

"Yes. He collects souls, Teresa, and he wants mine. He would have taken yours and the detective's if I hadn't stopped him. He was there at the start, but when I defended myself, he disappeared."

Teresa clutched her chest. "Does that mean you killed them?"

Alona lowered her head. She had to tell Teresa the truth. "I prefer to say I defended myself, but that's what the detectives were referring to. Listen, Teresa, I like you. You're a good worker. I'm going to tell you something and if you decide you want to leave, I understand."

Teresa stood there, eyes wide and mouth open, still clutching her chest.

"I'm a Nephilim, Teresa. Do you know what that is?"

"No?"

"My mother was raped by a fallen angel over two thousand years ago."

Teresa stumbled backward. Alona rushed to catch her. She grabbed a stool and set it behind Teresa. "Sit down, Teresa."

Teresa nodded.

"Are you okay, Teresa?"

"You're telling me you're over two thousand years old?"

"Yes."

"And you're half human, half angel?"

"Yes."

"Are you a good angel?"

"Other than yesterday, have you ever seen me do something bad?"

"No."

"Just like most humans, I try to be good. That demon wants my soul, Teresa. My mother prayed for God to spare me if she raised me to serve the Lord God. So, I do. I just can't sit by while bad people take advantage of good people and bully them or hurt them. Not when I can do something about it."

Teresa nodded. "So, you basically saved me and Detective Elena from being killed."

"Yes, because they couldn't have you identify them in a court of law now, could they?"

"I didn't think about that."

"I haven't told anyone else that I'm a Nephilim, so don't say anything, okay?"

"Do you have other super powers?"

"Other than my super strength, I can move super-fast, like a blur, and I can grow to sixteen feet."

"Cool."

"So, are you staying?"

"Sure, now that I know I'm working for a super hero, and I know your true identity."

"I'm not a super hero and I've only changed my name once."

"What is your real name?

"Noura Hashim."

"Well, Noura Hashim, you have super powers and you're my hero for saving my soul."

Alona gave Teresa a hug. "Thanks Teresa, but don't tell anyone. It's our secret, okay?"

"Cool, now I'm the sidekick who knows your secret identity."

Just then, the door chimed as someone entered. Alona glanced toward the door and saw Luke. Her heart rate kicked up a little.

"Hello, Luke!" she said.

"Are you ready for your lesson?" he asked.

She turned to Teresa. "Can you handle everything? Will you be all right?"

"Sure. I'm good."

Alona left with Luke. After telling Teresa her deep, dark secret, maybe she could tell Luke. He held her hand as they walked to the studio. She felt excited and enjoyed holding his hand. She didn't remember doing that with any of her past loves. Luke was different and he was beginning to grow on her.

She changed into her Gi and demonstrated all the positions Luke had taught her. Then he had her do the punches and kicks while he defended against them.

"Now, I'm going to try some things and I want you to counter the punches and kicks so I can see what you remember."

They had done this just yesterday, she thought.

"Today, we are going to get physical," he said.

"Hmm, I like the sound of that," she smiled.

Luke threw some punches on her arms. She defended

against them and gave him back the same thing, but she held back her full strength. But when he did some kicks, things got rougher. She continued to defend against them but gave him back the same thing he dished out to her.

She actually enjoyed this challenge, trying to remember all the ways to defend against the punches and kicks.

When the time came to an end, she told Luke about her visit from the detectives.

"I was afraid of that," he said.

"What do you mean?"

"I saw the body bags coming out of the office."

She reached out and touched his arms. "I don't...I... Luke, I'm a Nephilim."

He smiled.

She blinked. "I thought you'd be upset. Do you know what a Nephilim is?"

"Yes. I'm glad you told me."

"There's something else."

"What's that?"

"There was another body that wasn't there."

Luke raised his eyebrows.

"I fought the demon, Luke. He's been tracking me for years. He arranged the abduction. I don't think Teresa or detective Elena would be alive today if I hadn't stopped those men."

He reached out and hugged her. Tight. "This is a good start."

She felt her emotions spike upward. She was excited and happy, but his touch made her want him. She wanted to kiss him and feel him inside her. Was that too much to hope for? A normal, loving relationship with a man? When she felt his erection move against her belly, she knew he felt the same way. Or, at least, she'd like to think that.

"Uh, this may be a good time to stop."

"Okay?" She was disappointed when he pulled away. "Do you want me to make your favorite sandwich?"

"Yes. I'll come down in a few minutes and pick it up, if that's okay?"

This was new. Did she turn him on so much he couldn't shake the erection? "Sure." She left a little disappointed but elated that she had that kind of reaction from him.

By the time she had finished Luke's sandwich, it got busy. They had a line to the door, so Alona pitched in with the sandwiches to speed things up. Finally, Detective Cummings was at the counter.

"Hello Detective Cummings, how are you?" Alona asked.

"After what we've been through, call me Elena." Elena ordered her sandwich and Alona started it while they chatted.

"How are you both doing?" Elena asked.

"Tell her," Teresa said.

"Tell me what?" Elena asked.

"I need some help. Do you know any lawyers?" Alona asked. "I have one for a previous incident in the park, but I don't know if he handles things like what we just went through."

"Have they charged you with anything yet?"

"No, but they alluded to it."

Elena fumbled through her purse. "I have two brothers-in-law who are lawyers." She pulled out two cards. "Here, call them. They are both good people. And this one," she pointed to Rick Johnson, "was a cop and is now a lawyer, so he knows the ins and outs of both sides."

"Bless you. Thank you," Alona said.

"Will you be all right?" Elena asked.

"I hope so. I don't want to leave and start over. I like it

here." She just couldn't go to prison, not for life. Especially living as long as she had already.

"Why would you do that?"

"The warehouse... I defended myself, but I should have used the methods that Luke showed me. Instead, I reverted to my old ways."

Elena touched her arm. "I know you defended yourself, Alona. If you need me for anything, call me." Elena pulled out her own card and handed it to Alona.

"Thank you," Alona said. She watched Elena leave the shop. Then she glanced at the two cards. "I think I'll call this lawyer now," she said to Teresa. Since it was slow, she would take advantage of the time. She dialed the number of the lawyer Elena said had been a cop. She made an appointment with his office. When she got off the phone, she realized the other lawyer was the same one she had already seen about the attack in the park. *Oh, boy. Well, at least they worked for the same firm. I need all the help I can get. Especially if they figure I had anything to do with the thug in the garage.*

Luke sat with Elena in his small studio. "She's having a hard time changing old ways. She hesitates just enough that she could get hurt or revert to her old way of fighting. Now she's dealing with the law in the matter of defending herself," he said. But he was glad Alona was finally sharing her feelings with him.

"Does she know you're an angel?" Elena asked.

"Not yet."

"Maybe it's time you took her training up a notch."

"What do you mean?"

"Whenever she reverts to her old ways, give it back to

her so she can see what she's doing. Maybe that will force her to rethink how she reacts."

"If I do that, she will know I'm an angel."

"Is knowing so bad? I knew Pete was an angel when I first worked with him. I think I'm still good. I knew his strengths at the beginning and we worked well together. We still do and we get along great. He was recently injured on the job, though."

"Can he still heal himself?"

"Yes. In fact, he can still do many things except fight a demon and go invisible."

"Which demon?"

"The one that had something to do with the burglaries on this street. I think he's tied into this security company that will be installing the security system in my business next door."

Luke straightened.

"Will you still be able to watch them for me on Wednesday night?"

"Yes. I'll have to work something out, but yes, I'll do it." It had to be Raum. He's the one that had been tracking Alona for years. And Raum was the one she fought the other day. But Matthias' sudden disappearance would have to be explained unless he told her the truth by then.

"Good. I'll either be staking out the place or driving around on patrol. I hope to have a backup as well."

"You know you won't be able to stop the demon yourself?"

"Yes, I know. That's why I need your help. Pete is willing to help me, but he said only an angel can chain up a demon."

"He's right. You'll need to call on a legion of angels for

Wednesday night. That's the only backup you'll really need."

"Thanks, Luke." She stood to leave.

"One more thing," he said. He stood and walked her to the door of his office.

"Yes?"

"You had some furniture delivered on Friday. I went ahead and let them in for you."

"Oh, my goodness! I forgot all about it. I had a family emergency and left town. How did you get inside?"

"I can go through walls, remember? I made myself invisible and went in through the back door and opened the front door from the inside."

"Thank you so much, Luke. You know, Alona is really worried about this case with the warehouse?"

"Yes. I knew you could help her with a lawyer. I'm afraid the warehouse is not her only problem, though."

"What do you mean?"

"Alona is just starting to trust me. When she is able to tell me everything, then she will be ready to confide in you as well. I'll let her tell you her side of the story."

"Thanks again," Elena said. She left and headed toward her new office.

He leaned against the door. Now it was up to him. He couldn't jeopardize her safety with the demon still involved. Tomorrow would be an interesting training session. It would also determine whether or not they still went on the date. Should he tell her during training? It might be a good way for her to work out any anger issues.

It had been a long day and Alona was ready to go home. She looked forward to seeing Matthias and her heart felt glad. In fact, she had been happier than she had been in a long time just since meeting Luke and having Matthias in her life. And she wanted more of Luke in her life.

Her training with Luke was challenging today and she liked it. She didn't feel that the Mui Thai was second nature to her yet. She had several centuries of previous habits to undo. Or at least change her way of thinking. She never really had any training before. She just instinctively grew to her sixteen-foot self and choked the bad guys. If her height didn't scare them away, then they would continue their bad habits and they needed to be gone. She had seen that behavior enough to know that evil people didn't change because they didn't want to. Sometimes, she could see or feel the aura of good people. But the bad ones gave off a different frequency and she could feel that too.

She took extra time walking Matthias today. She threw the ball for him in the park, and he chased it, bringing it back to her and waiting for her to throw it again. She loved that. She let him lick her afterward. Hey, kisses from dogs were better than no kisses at all. Then she remembered the sweet kiss against her forehead when Luke tried to calm her down. The thought made her smile.

She fixed both of them some fresh food. Matthias especially liked eating real food instead of his dog food. He gave her more kisses. After her last walk with Matthias, she decided to have a talk with him.

"You know, Matthias, I've talked about Luke before. Tomorrow, we have a date. I'm not sure when we will go out. I'll find out something tomorrow at our training. But I want you to know, that I still love you, no matter what. I'd love to have a relationship with Luke. And I hope he likes you as well. But I don't want you to think that because I like Luke, a lot, that I like you less. Do you understand, boy?"

Matthias barked.

"I take that as a yes. I'm hoping I can get him to come home with me so you can meet him. His hair is so much like yours." She petted his fine, soft hair. "And he has brown eyes like you. And he's quite handsome."

Matthias barked.

"Oh, have you seen him?"

Matthias barked.

"Do you know Luke?"

Matthias barked.

Telepathically, she asked him. *'How do you know Luke?'*

Matthias repositioned himself so he was sitting, facing her. He put his paw on her knee. *'Because I am Luke.'*

Her eyes widened as she looked into Matthias' eyes. *'You are Luke?'*

'Yes.'

She cocked her head. *'How is that possible?'*

Matthias transformed into Luke before her eyes. His hand was on her knee as she sat on the couch.

"No!" She stood up.

Luke stood up. He held her arms to keep her facing him. "I understand if you don't want to see either of us again."

"What are you?"

"You sensed it long ago that I am a spiritual being. I am an angel. I was sent to find you and determine whether or not you had a good heart."

"I serve the Lord, God Almighty," she said.

"Yes, I know that now. And I sensed it once I found you."

"What are you here for?"

"If you had an evil heart, I was to destroy you. But I sensed Raum was after you as well."

"The demon?"

"Yes. I remained to protect you from him. He will try again to steal your soul."

"How long have you been Matthias?"

"The whole time."

"You heard everything I said? You saw me naked? You slept in my bed?"

Each accusation got louder and louder. He lowered his head. "Guilty as charged."

She covered her mouth. Her eyes watered. "I think you should leave."

He removed his hands from her arms. "I'm sorry if I offended you, Noura Hashim. I really do care about you." Then, he was gone.

8

―――――

Chapter Eight

Luke remained invisible but continued to monitor Alona's responses. He should have remained in spirit form the whole time, but he couldn't get an honest read of her personality. She was always alone except in her shop. People oftentimes act differently in their work environments than their home environments. Had he remained in spirit form, he wouldn't have had to deal with these human emotions. He did enjoy experiencing them, though.

He watched as Alona wiped her eyes and went into the kitchen. He watched her rummage through her cabinets, as if she searched for something. Finally, she pulled out a bottle that had been buried in the back of the tallest cabinet. She set it on the counter and retrieved a wine glass. He looked closer. Ah, a bottle of wine.

He watched her open the wine and pour herself a glass. Then, she took the wine glass and bottle and walked to the bathroom. She set them on the counter and ran water for the bath. She leaned on the counter and sipped her wine, watching the water fill the tub. Then, she slowly undressed. He enjoyed this part, but not as much as he did as Matthias. He smiled, remembering how he felt the first time he watched her take a shower. His emotions were strong then, but the same feelings were no longer present in his spirit form. If he had been with her as Luke, he would have helped her undress. He would have caressed her skin and kissed it. Who was he kidding? He would never get that chance now.

She poured a liquid into the running water and bubbles formed. Alona brought the wine bottle and glass to the edge of the tub, then she stepped inside. She stretched her long, naked form the length of the container and sank under the foam. Her head popped up. Alona straightened and reached for her glass, then refilled it with more wine.

He would remain in his spirit form, watching over her as he had been during the day. He would pop in and out of her reality when he needed to keep her safe. Once he took care of Raum, he would be out of her life.

Since Alona was half human, half angel, she never had a guardian angel. He was the closest thing to that. She really needed help with her fighting style, though. He was alerted to her whereabouts when she finished off the criminal in the parking garage. It was a matter of time before the police figured out she was the same person who destroyed the warehouse office. As far as the men in the park attack, her lawyer will be able to connect the dots soon enough. All he needed was a motive and since it was a spiritual motive, that would be hard to prove.

Alona took another sip of her wine and realized she was out. She lifted the bottle to pour another glass and it was empty. She shivered. *When did the water get cold?*

She stood and towel-dried herself off. She dressed for bed. She missed having Matthias here to talk to. The place felt lonely. She set her alarm and realized it was after 1:00 a.m. She never stayed up that late.

She tossed and turned, thinking of Matthias and the look on his face when he told her he was Luke. Then Luke's face came to mind, looking hurt with her words. *What about her feelings? Hadn't she been hurt, too?*

She awoke tired and rolled over to Matthias' side of the bed, but he wasn't there. An emptiness formed in her gut. Everything seemed to be going great until last night. She dressed and jumped into her morning routine. She hesitated before doing the exercises Luke taught her. She felt her strength had increased since she added them, and she could still use the techniques. What the heck, she did the exercises anyway. Not everything about Luke was bad. Sure, she felt betrayed, but he had helped her. Then she realized it was Luke who had saved her life in the park as Matthias when he took on those two men.

And he had slept with her! Although he looked and acted like a dog, he had his paws and his head on top of her each morning. *What a dirty dog!* But Matthias had brought a little happiness into her life, and she needed that. She didn't feel as lonely with him around. She even looked forward to seeing him each day. She missed Matthias.

After she finished her routine, she didn't feel like eating, so she dressed for the day. While she brushed her hair, she realized her eyes looked tired. Dark circles had formed under her eyes. Since she didn't wear makeup, she had no way to disguise the circles. Great!

Alona drove on to the shop, stopping at the bank to make her deposit. Today was payday for her and Teresa. By the time she got to the parking garage, there were no other cars there.

That's odd. She glanced at her phone. "Oh my gosh! I'm an hour early?" She realized that without Matthias in her life to walk each morning, her whole routine had changed overnight. Well, she was here now, she might as well get started.

She had everything prepped and ready for the day, but it was still early. She put on a pot of coffee. Since she hadn't been hungry earlier, she thought maybe she would be hungry now, but this emptiness inside her wasn't hunger. It was missing her Matthias. She would never see him again. And Luke? He had grown on her too. Her eyes watered at the thought. Her only happiness lately had come from both of them, and she sent them away.

Finally, when Teresa arrived, she perked up a little. Someone to talk to. "Good morning," Alona said.

"Hey, what's wrong? You look tired," Teresa said.

"I went to bed late and I couldn't sleep," she said.

"Something else is wrong, I can tell," she said.

"My dog, Matthias, is gone."

"Gone? Where? What happened?"

Alona realized she had confided in Teresa yesterday and she would continue to tell her the truth. She reached out to touch Teresa's shoulder. "You know what, since I told you the truth yesterday, I'm not going to lie to you anymore. Yes, Matthias is gone but that's because he really wasn't a dog after all."

Teresa grabbed a stool. "I think I better sit down for this one. So, what are you saying?"

"Matthias is Luke and Luke is an angel." Alona let out a

breath she didn't know she was holding. Relief washed over her.

"Luke is a shape-shifter?"

"Well, yes. I guess you could say that."

"This is so cool! I work for a super hero with a shape-shifting boyfriend!"

"Luke is not my boyfriend," she said. Although she did like the sound of that. "I asked him to leave yesterday when I found out."

"You did what?"

"He's seen me naked. He heard all my confessions about Luke. How creepy is that?"

"Hey, if he didn't like you, would he still come around as Luke?" Teresa asked.

Alona thought about that. All her confessions to Matthias were about her past or about Luke. And Luke did give her personal attention. There was no one else in the class. He hugged her like no one had ever hugged her before. Her arms ached for his touch at the thought of it. He even had erections after each hug, so she turned him on as a man. And he turned her on as a woman. And his hugs were long, warm hugs. "He was tracking me to make sure I was a good Nephilim."

"And did you prove yourself to him?" Teresa asked.

"I guess so. He said he would have had to destroy me if I was evil."

"There you go. Why don't you see if he's at the studio? Maybe he'll give you another lesson?"

"I don't know. Why would he?"

"Well, he hasn't finished your training, has he? Besides, don't you two have a date tonight?"

"We did. I think that's all off now."

"Why?"

"Because I told him to leave, and he did."

"Are you sure? Maybe he didn't leave," Teresa said.

"What do you mean?"

"Well, most people can't see angels because they're invisible, right? But you got to touch one and see one. How cool is that?"

"You saw him, too."

"Yes, but I work with you. How could he show himself to you and not me. That would have been more suspicious, don't you think?"

"Hmm." Alona glanced at her phone. It was early enough for a lesson. "I think I'll walk to the studio and see if he's there," she said.

"Good. I got this," Teresa said. She gave a thumbs up sign.

Alona headed in the direction of the Martial Arts Academy. Teresa got her thinking. She hadn't thought of invisibility before. She certainly couldn't do that herself. Had Luke remained in her home after she asked him to leave? She wanted some answers. She pushed open the door to the studio.

"Hello, is Luke in this morning?" she asked.

"I'm sorry, he hasn't—"

Luke stepped out from his office. "Hello Alona. Come on in," he gestured. He smiled as he held the door open for her and she went inside.

Once the door was closed, she got in his face. "When I told you to leave yesterday, did you?"

"Do you know what a guardian angel is?"

"You didn't answer my question." She poked him in the chest, moving closer. Luke backed up just a tad.

"A guardian angel is with you twenty-four seven. He sees everything you do and hears everything you say. And he knows what you think and feel."

"Are you telling me you watched me again last night?"

"I am the closest thing you have to a guardian angel, Alona. I have been watching you for some time since I became Matthias."

Alona took a deep breath and swung at Luke's face, but he was faster and blocked her with his arm. She grew to ceiling height, banging her head. She rubbed her head and watched him match her height.

"What are you doing, Noura? I taught you a better way to fight."

She reached for his neck, and he did the same to her. "Stop calling me Noura," she said. She squeezed his neck hard. His grip was strong, too.

"We will both pass out before we hurt each other," he said. He knocked her hand away with a punch.

She shrank to her regular six-foot height and used one of her kicks. Luke shrank down as well, but blocked her kick and threw a punch, catching her off guard. She punched back and then kicked Luke. The two of them continued sparring, but she was able to use everything Luke taught her. She was angry and wanted to hurt him. Luke countered everything she threw at him. She surprised herself by countering all his moves.

She had come here dressed in nice clothes and didn't have a chance to change into the Gi he kept for her. The clothes hindered some of her movements, but she was able to keep up.

'Why did you lie to me?' she sent him telepathically.

"I didn't lie to you, Noura. I just didn't tell you everything.'

'You invaded my privacy!'

'Most people don't even know they have a guardian angel and they are all watched, just the same.'

Somehow Luke was able to block her last punch and grabbed her arm. He spun her around against his chest and wrapped both arms around her so that her back was against his chest. He held her tight.

'Let me go!' Suddenly, she felt waves of calm go through her body.

'Noura, forgive me. I didn't mean to hurt you. I'm here to protect you from the demon, Raum.' His mouth was close to her ear and his breath sent tingles throughout her body.

'I changed my name to Alona centuries ago.' She twisted slightly in his arms. His hold was tighter than his normal hugs.

'I like the name, Noura Hashim, Light Destroys Evil.'

'Please,' she said.

'Please what?'

'Why are you torturing me?'

'I'm not torturing you. I'm trying to calm you down.'

She took in a deep breath and then let it out slowly.

'Can you forgive me, Alona? You won't be able to get rid of me.'

Her body sagged. She felt defeated, but she really liked having him close to her. 'I forgive you, Luke.'

He loosened his grip on her and she was able to face him.

"Can you forgive me?" she asked out loud. She reached around his back to hug him.

"Of course."

"I miss Matthias," she confessed. His arms were still around her.

His eyes widened. "Not me?"

"Well, I haven't slept with you or kissed you yet."

He hugged her the way he had before. "Well, we can always fix that." Then, as usual, she felt his erection against her belly.

"And I can help you fix that," she said. She waggled her eyebrow.

He lifted her chin and kissed her. It started out sweet and went straight to hot in a matter of seconds. Then he stopped, leaning his forehead against hers.

"Are we still going out tonight?" she asked. She wanted more of his kisses. He had just wet her appetite.

"I want to if you want to," he said.

"Yes, I want to," she said.

"Where would you like to go?"

"Surprise me."

Alona straightened her clothes and ran a hand through her hair before leaving his studio. She was excited about tonight. Whatever Luke had done to her had calmed her down. Maybe things would go back to some type of normal, or maybe her life would be changed forever.

"There you are! I was getting worried about you. You were gone longer than normal," Teresa said.

"I had some things to work out with Luke. I forgave him and he forgave me."

"He forgave you? What did you do to him?"

"Well, I turned my training into a real fight. He's very strong. I think he held back a little."

"You fought an angel?"

"And so did he," she said.

"Oh yeah, right! Well, are things good between you?"

"I think so, yes. I'll let you know on Monday."

"You're going to make me wait until Monday?"

"Yes, I am. And you can tell me about your Renaldo."

"Deal!"

Alona moved to the counter and put on her apron. Then after washing her hands, she started making Luke's favorite sandwich.

Luke smiled at the thought of going out with Alona. He had to be careful. His heart wanted her like a man wanted a woman, but he had things to do as an angel. He couldn't be compromised. He couldn't jeopardize Alona when things were getting dangerous with Raum still in the picture.

He waited long enough for his erection to go away, then headed to Alona's shop. He knew just the place to take her for their date. He picked up his sandwich. He wanted to chit chat with her and Teresa, but the two had gotten busy. He hurried out of the shop and headed back to his studio. He just hoped he could enjoy the time with Alona without crossing the line.

Just before closing time, Luke headed back to Alona's shop. "Hello, ladies. Did you have a good day?"

"Yes, we did," Alona said.

"We were just locking up," Teresa said.

"I came to walk you to the parking garage."

"That's thoughtful of you," Alona said.

"My pleasure." Luke's smile dazzled her.

"So where are you two going tonight?" Teresa asked. She stepped outside on the front sidewalk.

"It's a surprise," Luke said. He joined Teresa on the sidewalk.

Alona smiled. She liked that idea. "Where are you and Renaldo going?" She joined them on the sidewalk.

"We like dancing, so we're going to a dance club on South Beach," Teresa said.

"Cool. I hope you both have a great time," Alona said. She locked the door and the three of them headed to the garage.

"We usually do."

Luke made sure Teresa was safely in her car and drove away before he said anything to her. "Do you have anything you want to lock in your car before we go?"

"I just have my purse."

"You won't need it tonight."

"Okay." She locked her purse in the trunk of her car then stood before Luke. "I'm all yours."

Luke pulled her close in a nice hug and whispered in her ear. "Hang on."

She put both arms around his neck. The next moment, they stood on a white, sandy beach, waves lapping at the shore. No other people were in sight. The sun was setting off to her right. "Where are we?"

"A beautiful beach in Florida."

"The beaches are always packed in Miami, but this water is lighter, more turquoise. It's beautiful."

"We aren't in Miami." Luke snapped his fingers and they both wore shorts and tank tops. *Hmm, he had a nice build, muscular, like an athlete, not a body builder. She liked that.*

Luke took her hand and together, they walked down the

beach toward the setting sun. Her bare feet sloshed through the ankle-deep, warm water.

"I haven't done this in centuries. I love it," she said.

"I've watched a lot of humans go on dates. This is a way to get to know someone before deciding whether or not you want to spend a lifetime with that person."

Her heart hitched. What was Luke getting at?

"I've spent many lifetimes watching people. Sometimes I've been a guardian angel, other times a warrior. Every now and then, I do both for one soul. I've tracked you since the day you were born, Alona, but never found you until recently."

"I moved around a lot," she said.

"You've changed your looks and name several times, haven't you?"

"Yes. I had to."

"How long have you been Alona Gabriel?"

9

———

Chapter Nine

W as Luke interrogating her, or did he genuinely want to get to know her? "I've been Alona Gabriel a little over two hundred years. It's too hard to change names anymore. You have to have identification, social security number, driver's license."

Luke stopped walking and bent down to retrieve something. He handed her a large seashell. "This is a conch shell," he said.

"Thank you. Our souvenir from our date," she said. She held onto it with her free hand while Luke held her other hand. They continued walking and sharing their past lives. She enjoyed his company and realized she had never done this with anyone else. She kept her past in her past from all her husbands and children. "I have been married several times. Too many to count, really. I've had dozens of children and watched them, along with all my husbands, grow old and die. So many times I would dye my hair gray and when the last child died, I moved away and changed my name.

People would always question why I didn't age. I couldn't answer those questions without creating more questions, so I moved. It's been over a hundred years since my last child died," she said.

"I don't know those feelings, Alona. I remained in spirit form unless I shifted into an animal. Even animals have feelings, and some are capable of expressing emotions."

"Like Matthias?"

"Exactly. I usually shift into a dog because they are the most expressive and I get to enjoy some of the emotions that way. So, in spirit form, I feel no emotions. But when I became Matthias, I knew I had to help you with your fighting style, so here I am."

"Are you experiencing human emotions now?" Her heart beat faster just thinking about her emotions toward him.

Luke stopped walking. He stepped close to her. "I am experiencing all kinds of emotions just holding your hand. It's very exciting." He caressed her face. She closed her eyes, enjoying his touch.

"Why did you close your eyes?"

"I like it when you touch me. I was enjoying it more without the visual senses, if that makes sense?"

"I want to explore more emotions with you, but one thing holds me back."

She wanted to explore those same emotions with him, too. "What's stopping you?"

"If I step over the line between Heaven and Earth, and love you like I want, I will lose my powers as an angel."

"All of them?"

"I think so. I've been meaning to speak to Pete again to see how many powers he still has."

"Why? Was Pete an angel, too?"

"Yes. He fell in love with Elena and gave up Heaven to live with her on Earth. He lost some of his powers right away."

"It wouldn't matter to me, Luke. I liked you even before I knew you were an angel."

"This is why you need me, Alona. I am the only one who can stop Raum. I have to chain him up and cast him back into the fires of hell."

"And after that?"

"What do you mean?"

"After you cast Raum into the fires of hell, what happens to you? To me? To us?"

Luke smiled that dazzling smile again. "Beautiful things."

He wrapped his arms around her from behind and they watched the most beautiful sunset. She leaned against him, her head against his neck. She felt comfort in his arms. This was all she could hope for now. She couldn't expect more from him until the demon was gone.

Luke took her by the hand and headed back to where they started their walk as the skies grew darker. The colors in the sky were spectacular with pinks, oranges, gold, and deep purple.

"I'm really enjoying this time with you, Luke," she said.

When they reached their starting point, Luke snapped his fingers and a table and two chairs appeared. There were gas lights surrounding the table, making a romantic scene. The table was filled with seafood dishes and a couple bottles of wine.

Luke pulled out a chair for her and they sat across from each other. He poured them a glass of wine each.

"This is lovely. I can honestly say I've never experienced a date like this."

"Good. I wanted this to be special."

While the two ate the scrumptious food, they continued their conversation. There was lobster, fried fish, shrimp, rice and broccoli. Even the white wine tasted great with the meal. She didn't want this to end.

When they were both full, Luke snapped his fingers and everything disappeared. He pulled her close and whispered in her ear, "Hang on."

She blinked a couple times and then they were sitting on a rooftop in a big city.

"Where are we now?" she asked.

"New York."

"What?"

"We can sit here and talk more while watching the traffic and lights of the city."

She scooted closer to him. "Put your arm around me, Luke."

"Are you cold?"

"No, I just like you touching me."

Luke wrapped his arm around her shoulder and she cuddled next to him. "Is kissing okay?" she asked.

"What do you mean?"

"You kissed me earlier and you seem to still have your powers. Can we do that?"

Luke wrapped both arms around her and whispered again, "Hold on."

In the next instant, they were inside her home.

"Now I know where we are."

Luke still held her in his arms, but they faced each other. He lifted her chin and kissed her sweetly on the lips. Like before, the kiss deepened, and her passions rose. He was a good kisser with a talented tongue. Just when the kiss was making her hot, he stopped.

'*No! Don't stop now,*' she sent telepathically.

'*I don't think I can stop myself if we go any further,*' he sent back to her.

'*I would be fine cuddling and watching a movie with you,*' she said telepathically.

She sat between his legs while he wrapped his arms around her. They snuggled and watched a romantic movie until she got sleepy.

"You need your sleep. You didn't sleep well last night," he said.

"Stay with me, Luke."

"You have two options. One is I stay in spirit form, the other is I stay as Matthias."

"Definitely Matthias." She turned to kiss his cheek and then he was Matthias. "Okay, Matthias, let's go to bed." She went to the bathroom and did her nightly routine, washing her face and brushing her teeth. She changed into her pjs and then crawled into bed. She reached to turn off the light and Matthias jumped off the bed. She watched him push the bathroom door open with his nose and walked inside. She heard him peeing and wondered where he was doing that. Before she could get out of bed, she heard the toilet flush. Then Matthias came out of the bathroom and jumped onto the bed.

'*Well, now that I know you can do that, we can save ourselves a morning walk.*'

Matthias barked.

She kissed his face, then lay down on her pillow, putting her arm around him. '*I love you Matthias.*' Then she leaned close and kissed his face again. '*I love you, Luke.*'

When Alona awoke, Matthias' head was on her belly. She glanced at him and petted his head. "Good morning, Matthias," she said.

He raised his head, and she moved off the bed, taking care of her morning needs. She quickly changed into her workout clothes. When she was through, Matthias jumped off the bed and walked into the bathroom and closed the door. Alona scratched her head. She wasn't sure what to expect today, so she headed to the workout room.

She began her regular workout and saw Luke leaning against the door frame, arms crossed, watching her.

"You can join me, if you like."

"Don't mind if I do," he said.

While Alona did the regular workout, Luke did the exercises for Mui Thai. When she finished, she joined him.

"Today, I want to teach you some skills you need to have," Luke said. *She doesn't realize how many gifts she has.*

"Oh? What kind of skills?"

"I'll teach you how to use the Armor of God to protect yourself." *She needs this more than she realizes.*

"The Armor of God?"

"Yes, haven't you used it before?"

"No. I thought it was something to wear."

"It is, but you'll need to familiarize yourself with it. We should do that outside." *This training was more important than the Mui Thai when it comes to demons.*

"The park is busy on Saturdays," she said.

"I know lots of places we can practice." He pulled her close, hugging her tight. He loved touching her, but it was getting harder not to do it. She hugged him back. His body instantly reacted. "Hang on," he whispered in her ear. He thought of an empty field in the middle of nowhere, and they were there. Now, he had to keep his mind on his work. He released her. "Do you know how to put on the Armor of God?"

"Yes, but it's been a while," she said.

Luke thought his on. He watched her go through the prayer, putting on one item at a time.

"How can I see yours and not mine?" she asked.

He blinked and hers was visible. He could see his shield was much larger than hers. He stepped closer. "You need to visualize this armor and say 'manifest,' for it to manifest. Try it." He blinked and her armor was invisible again.

She closed her eyes. Then she had on the armor once more.

She opened her eyes. "I didn't know I could do that."

"I'll teach you more things later. Right now, hold your shield of faith up, like this." He demonstrated for her. She held hers up.

"This is heavy," she said.

"Yes, that's why you have to practice as well as doing those exercises. Now, hold your sword up like this," he said. He demonstrated again. Then he showed her different ways to wield the sword. "Now, let's practice." They spent a good hour or so just practicing with the sword and holding the shield to defend against an opponent's sword.

"I'm getting hungry, aren't you?" she asked.

"Yes, I am." She must have heard his stomach growl. That was a new thing for him. He wasn't used to eating on a regular basis, but as long as he remained in human form, he had to feed this body.

"Let's go home and eat. We can come back and practice later, can't we?"

"Yes, we can." He liked that idea. He blinked and his armor was gone.

"How did you do that?"

"Just imagine yourself not wearing the armor."

She closed her eyes. Instantly, the armor was gone.

"You're getting the hang of it." He pulled her close.

"I really love this part," she said.

"Oh, you do?"

"Yes. I get to hold you and you hold me."

He pictured the inside of her kitchen, and they were there. One day, he would hold her and not have to let her go. He kissed her neck below her ear. Her arms grew tighter around him.

"If you keep that up, I will let you have your way with me," she said.

"Promise?"

She poked him in the chest. "Help me fix breakfast."

He watched her get some utensils out and heat up one of the pans. He had seen people cook before and he was a fast learner. When he realized what she was about to cook, he jumped in and helped her.

He hastily set the table and she served the eggs, bacon and toast. "This is really good. I've seen it cooked lots of times, but I've never eaten eggs before."

"I'm glad you like it. It's more fun when I have help in the kitchen."

He helped her clean up after breakfast. Then he showed Alona more things she didn't know she could do, like going invisible. She was able to hold it for a minute. That could give her enough time to escape, since she was very fast. Maybe she could increase the time with practice. She already had a lot of things to work on. He didn't want to discourage her.

He tried to show her how to teleport, but that was too difficult. Maybe she really didn't have that skill. Or maybe, she needed to master manifesting first?

"I think we'll work on manifesting things," he said. "That may help you later with teleporting."

Alona manifested small things. "That's good, it's a start," he said. They practiced for a couple hours. "Maybe with more practice, you could manifest a meal tonight," he said.

"Well, I don't mind cooking something for you."

"Really? I haven't ever had anyone do that for me but you. I love those sandwiches you make for me every day."

"How about a steak? Matthias likes them."

"Yes, I did enjoy that. Let's work on the Armor of God before cooking dinner," he said.

"Sure. Let me take out a couple of steaks."

He took her back to the field they were at this morning. They practiced for another hour or so.

"How can I get a big shield like you have?" she asked.

"Visualize it then manifest it," he said.

She did. "This is even heavier than the other."

"Yes, but it offers you more protection. Let's practice a little more with this shield." They worked a little longer, using the shield for deflecting sword attacks. He showed her how to hold it to protect her body from fire darts. When it was time to go, he held her tight. This was getting harder for him. Each touch brought him to the brink. How long could he hold out this way? Once they were back in her kitchen, she kissed his neck.

"I couldn't resist. You are so yummy," she said.

"Yummy?"

She kissed his neck again, then licked him.

His heart rate shot up. "If you continue that, Matthias will be eating dinner with you."

"I'm sorry."

He took her hand. "Don't be. I enjoy your touch as well. I'm just having problems controlling these human emotions right now."

"Do you think I'm not?" she asked. "This is hard for me not to touch you more."

Alona tried to control her emotions as well, but it was difficult. She and Luke spent the remainder of the day grilling steaks and preparing a meal without touching each other.

She pulled out some old board games after dinner and they played a couple for some time before cuddling on the couch and watching a sci-fi movie. She let Luke pick out the movie since she picked out the last one.

When it was time for bed, she snuggled next to Matthias and dreamed of Luke.

The next day was Sunday, and it was more of the same. They practiced in the field for a couple hours on swordplay and using the shield to defend, since she took the day off from her regular exercise routine. But she got a harder workout in the field.

She was also getting the hang of manifesting things and going invisible. This time, she was able to stay invisible for up to two minutes. With the teleportation, she got as far as invisibility but nothing else. "I guess I wasn't meant to teleport," she said.

Luke lifted her chin. "This is why you need me."

She wanted to kiss him, but he put a finger against her lips. "Be strong for me."

It was getting harder to be strong while Luke was there, but she didn't like the alternative.

Monday morning, Alona got up to do her exercise routine after sleeping with Matthias. He joined her as Luke and the two of them finished the two workouts, ate breakfast and got dressed for the day.

"You'll get to ride in my car to the shop this morning," she said.

"You forgot, we didn't arrive here in your car," Luke said.

Her eyes widened. Luke pulled her toward himself. "Hang on," he whispered. She did and in the next instant, they stood beside her car. She retrieved her purse and walked to the shop with Luke holding her hand.

"You know, that saves a lot of gas. We should do that more often."

Luke smiled at her and squeezed her hand a little. Once they were in her shop, Luke helped her prepare the veggies for the sandwiches. Before it was almost time for Teresa to arrive, she turned to Luke. "Could I have one kiss before you head to the studio?" she asked.

"To tell you the truth, I don't really go to the studio except to work with you."

"You don't?"

"No. I remain invisible here with you."

"Really? You've been doing that all this time?"

"Only since I discovered where you were."

"Were you here before the demon showed up?"

"He was here?" *She was finally admitting it.*

"Yes, but it's been a while. Actually, it was about the time all the robberies occurred in the neighborhood."

"I found you after that. But that means he knows where you are."

"Are we still training today?"

"Certainly. I can't have you forgetting Mui Thai, now, can I?"

"You've been working me out a lot lately."

"I'm trying to get your angel self into shape."

"Is it working?"

He put his hands on her waist and pulled her close. "I'd say it's working out nicely."

"How about that kiss?"

Luke kissed her with more passion than he had before. Her arms were around him, pressing his body against hers. He tightened his grip on her until his erection stopped everything. She wanted more of him, but he was gone. She licked her lips. One of these days, she would have Luke, all of him, and she would make up for lost time.

10

———

Chapter Ten

"Good morning!" Teresa said.

"Good morning, yourself," Alona said. "Tell me about your weekend."

"Renaldo proposed to me on the dance floor!"

"Oh, my, gosh!" Alona hugged Teresa. "I am so happy for you! Have you planned a date yet?"

"Oh, no. I was so excited that he asked me. We celebrated all weekend long. We're going to talk about the date next weekend."

"Did he give you a ring?"

"Oh, I almost forgot." She showed off the diamond Renaldo had picked out for her.

"This is gorgeous. I love it. Do you still plan on working for me?"

"Of course, but I will need some time off for a honeymoon."

"You got it. Just let me know when."

Alona hugged her again.

"What about you?"

"What do you mean?" Alona asked.

"How was your date? Where did he take you?"

"It was unlike any other date, Teresa. He took me to a private beach, and we walked into the sunset, holding hands."

"How romantic," Teresa said.

"Very. We talked about our pasts, then he served me a wonderful seafood dinner."

"He cooked for you?"

"He snapped his fingers, and the food was there. After that, he snapped his fingers again and we sat atop a tall building in New York, watching traffic and the lights until I realized that all I wanted was him."

"Oooh, then what?"

"He brought me home and we cuddled on the couch and watched a romantic movie."

"Did you have sex?"

"No, but the more I get to know him, the more I want him."

"Was it you or him?" Teresa asked.

"What do you mean?"

"Why haven't you, you know, had sex?"

"Do you know anything about angels, Teresa?"

"Uh, no, not really."

"Well, angels are spiritual beings, just like humans, and they have free will, but they belong to Heaven, while we belong to Earth. If he and I were to make love, he would give up Heaven and become Earthbound. He would lose his powers."

"Oh, man, that's awful. Why couldn't he keep his powers?"

"He has to choose between Heaven and Earth. He can't have both."

"Wow."

"Yeah, he's doing this to save me from the demon. Only an angel can bind up a demon and take him back to hell."

Teresa reached out and touched her arm. "He's doing this because he loves you. I've seen the way he looks at you."

She leaned against the counter, her arm propping up her chin. "Yes, I know. It's been hard for both of us."

The shop got busier earlier than usual. The next time Alona glanced at the clock it was 5:30 p.m. She realized she hadn't seen Luke or worked out with him. *Had something gone wrong?*

"Should I start putting things away, Alona?"

"Yes. It will take us thirty minutes to clean everything up after the day we've had. Hopefully, the crowd is done."

With both of them working on the cleanup, they finished with a few minutes to spare.

"Teresa, go ahead and put the closed sign up. I've got to call in a food order. You can leave if you want," she said.

"I'll stay so we can walk to the parking garage together. I feel safer that way," Teresa said.

Alona finished the order and the two of them walked to the garage.

"Something must be going on downtown for business to pick up like it did," Teresa said.

"I agree." Alona made sure Teresa was safe in her car before heading to her own vehicle.

Once she was inside, Luke sat beside her. "I missed you today," she said.

He took her hand and raised it to his lips, kissing it. "I missed you as well. To tell the truth, I'm really struggling with these human emotions, and I find it hard to keep my hands off you when I'm in the flesh. Matthias will keep you company for a while." Then Matthias sat beside her. He stood and licked her face.

She hugged Matthias. "I've missed you, too, Matthias. You need to sit while I drive, boy, so I can concentrate on the road." Matthias lay on the seat beside her.

"Since you've been with me all day, I guess you know how my day went, so there's nothing new to tell you." She drove home as usual. Then she fixed dinner for both of them. Now that she knew Luke was Matthias, she would cook for him like she cooked for herself. "No more dog food for Matthias," she said. Matthias wagged his tail. "I thought you'd like that idea."

After dinner, she cuddled with Matthias on the couch and watched a movie. Matthias continued to use her bathroom as a man and came out as a dog.

Later, when she went to bed, she snuggled with Matthias and fell asleep.

Tuesday started out differently than Monday, in that after she did her workout routine, she cooked breakfast for both her and Matthias. Then she and Matthias walked to her car, and they drove to the shop. Once she pulled into a parking spot, she hugged Matthias, and he licked her face. "I'm going to miss you today, Matthias." She kissed his face. "I miss you, too, Luke." Then he was gone.

The day was just as busy as Monday and everything started from the moment the shop sign said 'Open.'

At some point, Elena came in. "Hello ladies," Elena said.

"Oh, hello, Elena. I have an appointment with your brothers-in-law next week," Alona said.

"Good. That's a start. I'm sure they can help you."

"We've been hopping this week," Teresa said. "We had to put in an extra order for food, but it won't come in until tomorrow night."

"I'll take care of it, Teresa. It's not your fault we've been busy," Alona said.

The day continued to be busy until sometime after 5:30 p.m.

"Alona, since you are taking care of the food order, how about I come in earlier on Thursday to give you some time off?"

"Would you do that for me?"

"Sure. It's the least I can do since I'm not helping you put everything away."

"I think it's time I make you assistant manager around here. You already do everything I do except make the deposits and write the checks."

"Oooh, does that mean I get a raise?"

"Sure, why not. I've been meaning to take some time off anyway, so this will work out fine."

Cleanup was quick and they were able to get out of the shop by 6:15 p.m.

By the time Alona got into her car, Matthias was there, waiting for her. "Hey, boy! I missed you today." Matthias licked her face, and she hugged him back. "How about a walk today?"

Matthias barked.

Once they got home, she grabbed some toys and his leash and headed to the park. She let him run and she kept up with him. Then she tossed some toys for him to fetch. Finally, she sat down with him to have a chat.

"I don't know how much of this dog stuff you really like doing, I mean are you just acting the part?"

'No. As a dog, I enjoy these games. I enjoy running.'

"I know what you are doing for me, and I appreciate it, but I'm at the point where I want to hunt this demon down and kill him now."

'Be patient.'

"I know that's not easy for you either." She hugged him and kissed his face. "How about something to eat?"

Matthias barked. She walked him back to the house.

Once she had dinner started, her phone rang.

"Hello?"

"Hello, Alona, this is Juan Del Toro. I called to let you know your court case has been cancelled."

"What? Why is that?"

"Both men who attacked you were recently found dead."

"Dead? How did that happen?" Her heart beat faster.

"Apparently, they were killed in a recent incident at a warehouse. You must have heard about it on the news?"

Her heart pounded.

"I have connections with the Miami-Dade Police Department. There's an investigation ongoing about a murdered man in a downtown parking garage, as well as the North Miami PD's investigation in the warehouse murders."

"What have those got to do with me and my case?"

"I think we need to talk, Alona."

"Sure. When?" *How was she going to explain this?*

"First thing next week."

"I already have an appointment with Rick Johnson about something else next week."

"He's one of my partners and my brother-in-law. We'll just keep the same appointment and meet you together at that time."

"Okay, fine. See you then." She ended the call, and quickly finished cooking dinner. She ate at the coffee table so she could sit beside Matthias. "I'm in serious trouble, Matthias. The police are looking at these cases as murders. I defended myself from these thugs and they want to charge me with murder? I don't understand their thinking. When did honest people get charged with murder while defending themselves against known criminals?" Matthias licked her face.

"I need all the help I can get, Matthias. What should I do?"

'I will help you.'

She kissed his face and hugged him.

'This is why you need me.'

The next morning, Alona finished her exercises and went to fix breakfast for her and Matthias. She couldn't find him anywhere. "Matthias? Luke?"

'I am here,' Luke sent telepathically.

'Where's Matthias?'

'He's having problems with kissing you. I almost couldn't stop myself this morning.'

She remembered his prolonged licking and had almost wet her pants trying to get away from him.

'Don't leave me!'

'Never. I am here with you now. I will be with you all day at the shop.'

'I love you, Luke.'

'I love you, Alona.'

~

After prepping extra food for the day, Alona realized that the food would be tight today. They might even run out by the end of the day. If her order didn't come in like it was supposed to, they couldn't open for tomorrow.

She would also have to make a deposit first thing in the morning. When Teresa arrived, they had fifteen minutes before things got busy.

At one point, she had so many customers in her shop that she didn't recognize, she asked one of them. "What brings you to town?"

"Oh, we're at a convention down the street and lunch was on our own. We heard you had great sandwiches, so here we are."

"Why thank you for choosing us." In the future, she would check the hotels with conference rooms to give herself a heads up in the food department. She couldn't afford to run out of food.

By 5:30 p.m., things had slowed down a little. She and Teresa had things cleaned up and ready to close when the food truck pulled up.

"I'll get this, Teresa, if you will cover for me in the morning."

"Sure thing, Alona. Thanks bunches!" She watched Teresa leave as the delivery man brought in the cases of food. She quickly inventoried the boxes and then locked up after the driver left.

Alona opened the boxes, one at a time and dated the food before putting things away. Other than the food thawing out, there was no hurry since she wouldn't see either Matthias or Luke tonight. The thought of that prospect left her sad.

'*Is everything set on your end, Luke,*' Elena sent telepathically.

'*Yes, I'm in my studio next door, waiting.*' Luke bilocated to his studio. He didn't like doing this because he couldn't focus completely on either place. He had promised to help Elena and Pete with their investigation of the security company but the timing was bad, unless this was part of the evil plan Raum had all along.

Darkness fell across the area. Alona would be leaving soon, and he had to stop her. If he couldn't be with her, he didn't want her to go home alone.

Then, he felt it. The presence of something evil.

'*Luke, Alona has company,*' Elena sent telepathically.

He moved toward the door to allow Elena and Pete entrance into their shop. Once Elena entered, he left. He had to get to Alona and let her know he was here.

There, inside her shop was Alona, facing the front door and Raum, facing her. Luke remained invisible. "Who are you?" Alona asked.

"Raum. I've come to ask your help, Noura Hashim. It's taken me a couple thousand years to find you."

"Whatever you're selling, I'm not interested," she said.

"Oh, I know you're there, officers. There's no need to worry. I'm not interfering with anything."

'Officers? Who else was in this shop?' She couldn't see anyone else since it was totally dark behind Raum. 'Did he create this darkness?'

"You are trespassing. Now leave or I will have them arrest you," Alona said. If the police were really there, she hoped they could hear her.

"There isn't anything they can do to me, Noura. You should know that."

"You can leave. I don't want anything to do with you," she said.

"You haven't let me explain what I want with you, Noura," Raum said.

"I know what you are here for, and you can't have it."

"Well, if I can't have your cooperation and help, I'll just take their souls."

Alona immediately envisioned the armor of God and wore it. From her back entrance, a man walked in with the armor of God on as well. *Who is this guy? He must be good if he's wearing God's armor.*

"Oh, so you brought reinforcements?" Raum glanced around. She could make out two other figures behind Raum who also wore the armor of God. Raum shot out fire darts at all of them, but they fell away from the armor.

"You know why I've been searching for you all these years, don't you?"

"No! And I don't want to know," Alona said. The fire darts were so strong, she couldn't move forward. Suddenly, the room lit up. Above her head was a legion of angels, crowding into her shop, surrounding all of them. Everyone had on the armor of God.

"You are one of us," Raum said.

"No, I'm not. I serve the Lord, God Almighty. I will never serve your master!"

"Oh, but you will. I insist."

Raum shot huge, powerful fire darts at her, over and over. Her shield grew hot. She envisioned it larger, and it became larger, taking the blows, but the force of the darts pushed her back against a wall. She kept her shield up and realized the practice with Luke was no coincidence. He must have known something was about to happen.

She held her sword and stepped forward, but it was like pushing against hurricane force winds. She heard other voices. The man beside her tried to move forward as well. He took strong blows from Raum's darts. *Who was he and why was he helping her?*

When she was able to peek over her shield, she caught sight of Pete, wearing his armor of God. Elena wore hers as well as she moved toward Raum's back. Then everything stopped momentarily. She took a step forward and the fire darts started again. Then, it happened a couple more times. In between the stopping and starting, she saw Elena stab Raum from behind, paralyzing him for a brief few seconds. They were all helping her fight this demon!

With all four of them, Raum couldn't use his full force on her. Suddenly, she heard an angelic choir. She glanced up and saw Luke descending with chains. In a flash, he had Raum bound and covered with chains. The ceiling of her shop opened to Heaven. She watched as Luke carried Raum off with the legion of angels surrounding both of them.

She collapsed on her knees. Her shield and armor, gone.

Elena ran to her. "Are you all right?"

She struggled to prop herself up. She hadn't realized how much strength she used to fight Raum. "Thank you," she said.

Elena helped her off the floor. Pete and the other man remained vigilant in her shop.

"Sometimes demons have underlings that tag along," Pete said.

Elena had her arm around her, supporting her, while they walked to a stool. "He drained me," she said. "I've never felt this weak before."

"Have you ever fought a demon before?" Elena asked.

"No."

"Me neither. I think we did well for our first time," Elena said. "You were fantastic the way you held up under fire. I don't think I could have done that."

"Luke is an angel," Alona said.

"Yes, he told me."

"How long have you known?"

"A little before you did," Elena said. "He tried to protect you for as long as he could."

"Protect me from what? Raum?"

"I think so. He didn't want you hurt."

"I protected myself."

"Yes, but only an angel can chain up an evil spirit. We did this as a team. We worked well together."

"I think we're safe for now," Pete said.

"I'm Mike, a former angel, like Pete. In fact, Pete trained me to be a guardian angel." He reached his hand out to Alona and she shook it. "What gifts do you have?"

"I have my strength and speed, and I can grow to sixteen feet. Luke was teaching me martial arts and a few other skills," she said.

"That's a good skill to have. Keep up the work," Mike said.

"What's that?" Elena asked.

She heard it too. It was a scraping sound in the ceiling. She stretched to ceiling height and pushed open a tile. There was a cable being pushed through her ceiling. She grabbed the cable and pulled it into the shop. "What is this?" she asked.

"They are supposed to be installing security cameras in my office, several shops down," Elena said.

Pete rushed to the front door and headed outside.

"Stay here," Mike said. He rushed out the back door.

Elena made a motion with her finger to be quiet. She put her arm around her shoulder, while Alona held the cable in her hand.

She saw a police unit drive past her shop without the siren on. "What's going on?" she asked. Her strength was gradually coming back.

Elena explained that her original plan was to expose the security company as criminals, but since Alona had dispatched all of them in the warehouse, they had to put together another team. Elena wanted to know who was involved in this new team and why they were so secretive about the installation.

Then Luke was there. "Luke?" She went to him, and he hugged her. A nice long, warm hug. The kind of hug that led to other feelings. He pulled away slightly. "We have a lot of things to catch up on," he said.

"Yes, we do."

Luke turned to Elena. "Your police backup came through. Raum had your captain under his control. You'll find things will be somewhat normal after this."

"Where are Pete and Mike?"

"They are assisting the police. What you decide to do

after tonight, is up to you. Just know that Alona and I will be glad to assist you whenever the need arises."

"Thank you, Luke."

Luke snapped his fingers and everything in the shop went back to normal. All the food had been put away earlier, so just the furniture needed to be straightened. "If you leave now, I can lock up," Luke said.

Elena took her cue and left out the front door.

Luke had held onto Alona the whole time. She clung to him with both arms. Once Elena was gone, he kissed Alona like he had never kissed her before.

11

———

Chapter Eleven

His kiss was thorough, exploring her mouth, His tongue danced with hers. Every inch of his body vibrated at a higher frequency than before. He was no longer on the ground. He envisioned her home, and they were there, in her bed. He envisioned her naked flesh, and there she was, her warm body against his. Her arms wrapped around his back. Her legs twined with his.

He caressed her skin with his fingertips. He kissed and licked her flesh, tasting every bit of her. He wanted to make this moment last. While he enjoyed her, she did the same to him, licking and blowing on his moist flesh, kissing and caressing. His body tingled from her touch.

His shaft tightened from his arousal and Alona continued to torture him. He wanted her to want him, so he continued the suckling and kissing. He found the spot that made her jump from excitement and pleasure. He continued to caress her until she could take no more.

"Now, Luke! Please, now!"

He entered her flesh, enjoying all the sensations that went along with it. It was all he had imagined. He started a slow rhythm while she kissed his neck. Now he knew why she enjoyed that. The sensations sent him over the edge and his rhythm picked up on its own. She joined him, matching his rhythm until they both came together and then collapsed in ecstasy. Her arms tightened around him, and he tightened his arms around her. She kissed him tenderly.

He loved everything about her. "This was worth the wait," he said.

"Hmm. I can do this with you all night," she said.

"Would you?"

She rolled him over on his back. "Are you ready for round two?"

"I am, but this body needs to recover for a few more minutes."

"You certainly surprised me for a first timer," she said.

"I've learned from some of the best," he said.

"You pervert." She kissed him again.

"I couldn't help it. I was a guardian angel for several men."

"Well, I like your style."

After another round, she fell asleep in his arms. He knew this was where he belonged as well.

The next morning, Alona awoke with an arm over her breasts and a leg across her crotch. She glanced over and saw Luke smiling in his sleep. He was so cute, but she had to pee. She tried to move, and he caressed her breasts.

"I heard morning sex was even better than night sex," Luke said.

"Really? Well, it will have to wait until after I use the bathroom."

He let her up and she headed to the bathroom to relieve herself. When she came out, Luke was gone. "Luke?" She walked out into the living room. Luke walked through the front door, naked.

"Did you just walk outside like that?"

"No, I went out as Matthias. I had to pee as well."

"You walked through the door without opening it?"

"Yes." His eyes widened.

"You know what that means?" she asked.

He ran to her. "I still have my powers!" He picked her up and swung her around. "We need to try them all out," he said.

"Of course. So, you can go invisible, right?"

He went invisible and then came back.

"Good. What about teleportation?"

He snapped his fingers, and they were both dressed in shorts and t-shirts. He wrapped his arms around her, and she reciprocated. In the next instant, they were on the same beach from their date. "It looks like I'm still an angel."

She kissed him. "And you still taste like one, too."

"I don't understand why I still have my powers and angels like Pete and Mike lost their powers."

"Maybe because I'm half angel?"

"That might just be why, Alona. I'm not going to question it I'm going to enjoy it." He held her tight and in the next instant, they were in her home. He snapped his fingers, and they were naked. "Now, where were we?"

～

After another couple rounds, Alona showered and got dressed for the day. When she walked into the kitchen, Luke had prepared breakfast for both of them. "I've worked up an appetite. I thought you might be hungry as well."

"I'm hungrier than usual. Thanks, Luke."

After they ate, Alona cleaned up while Luke showered and dressed.

"What will you do today now that we conquered that demon?" she asked.

"I can remain in your shop and help you as a human or go invisible and be a guardian."

"What about our Mui Thai lessons?"

"I think we can do those here, in your workout room. There's enough room to do the Mui Thai."

She grabbed her purse and the deposit bags. "So, you're thinking of staying?"

"I would like to," he said. His brows raised.

She caressed his face. "I would like you to, as well. Since I'm going in late today, we'll skip the Mui Thai. I'll work out a plan tonight for tomorrow. Maybe we can teleport here to practice and then head back afterward."

"Excellent. Shall I teleport us today?"

"I need to stop at the bank on the way to the shop."

"Just think about which bank and we'll go," he said.

"Sure." In an instant, they were at her bank. Instead of using the drive through, they walked inside. She took care of the deposit and then once they were outside, he hugged her, and they were in the shop's back room.

"That was convenient. Just think of the gas I saved by not driving."

"It's the only way to travel."

"My favorite part is the hugging." He hugged her tight and she kissed him. "Now, I need to get to work," she said.

"Alona! I didn't hear you come in," Teresa said. "Oh, hi, Luke."

"Hello Teresa. I'm here to help today," he said.

"Great. Grab an apron. I'll let Alona train you. She's the best teacher."

"Yes, she is," he said.

Alona smiled at him and noticed the ceiling panel was left open from the night before. "I forgot about that ceiling tile," she said.

"Oh, I wondered what happened with that," Teresa said.

Since no one else was in the shop, Luke stretched up and put the wire back inside the ceiling and fixed the tile in place. Just after he finished, some customers came in.

Alona leaned close to Teresa. "We took out the demon last night and Luke still has his powers."

Teresa's eyes grew large, and she must have realized what Alona meant because a big smile grew across her face. She punched Alona in the arm. "It's about time."

Alona showed Luke how to run the register so she could help Teresa make sandwiches. It only took a few times ringing something up and Luke caught on. The three of them worked well together and were able to keep up with the extra customers.

While Alona helped Teresa, she was able to fill her in on what happened with the demon. Later, when it slowed down, Teresa asked Luke a question. "Won't they miss you in the Martial Arts Academy?"

"That was temporary only. I used a small office, converted to a classroom, just for Alona. I had no other students."

"So, you aren't teaching her martial arts anymore?" Teresa asked.

"On the contrary, we will convert her exercise room into

a Mui Thai training room. I want her to be able to feel so comfortable using Mui Thai that she will forget how she protected herself before," Luke said.

"How *did* you protect yourself before, Alona?"

"The only way I knew how. I would grow to sixteen feet and squeeze their necks or toss them around. It didn't end well for the bad guys," Alona said.

"We want to leave the bad guys for the police to take care of here on out, right, Alona?" Luke asked.

"If you insist."

Luke stood very close and lifted her chin. "I insist." Then he kissed her.

"Hmm, I can't argue with that, but I might need more persuasion," she winked.

"Customer," Teresa whispered.

At the end of the day, three people cleaning up made everything go so much faster. They were able to get out of there by six. Alona and Luke walked Teresa to her car and then teleported home.

Friday was more of the same at the shop and Alona worked out a schedule for the Mui Thai for ten in the morning, shortly after Teresa arrived. Alona would do her regular exercises in the mornings before going to the shop.

Then, she and Luke spent Saturday practicing manifesting and going invisible. They also did some sword and shield work in the field as before.

On Sunday, Luke took her back to the private beach and they held hands, walking into the sunset, sharing past memories.

Luke stopped and turned to face her. "I've decided I

want you in my life permanently. Will you marry me and be my wife and life partner?"

"Yes!" Alona reached her arms around his neck. They shared a tender kiss. "You know, this time will be my last time marrying anyone."

"I should hope so. I won't let anyone else have you." He took her left hand and kissed it. There on her finger was a beautiful diamond ring. She kissed him again and in the next instant, they were in her bed.

They made love over and over until they fell asleep from exhaustion. Alona held Luke in her arms, his head on her breasts, and his arms and legs wrapped around her. "This is why I need you, Luke."

He lifted his head. "And this is why I need you."

Monday morning, after the shop was open and Teresa arrived, Alona and Luke went to speak with the lawyers instead of doing Mui Thai. "Tell them the truth," Luke said. "We'll see how they handle it."

"I'm not sure how much they know since they are Elena's brothers-in-law. Certainly, they know Pete was an angel, right?"

"I'm not sure what they know, but we'll see when they call us in," Luke said. He sat next to Alona in the office lobby of the law firm.

Finally, both Juan and Rick came out to greet them and they both stood.

"Hello, you must be Alona Gabriel?" Rick said. He reached his hand out to shake hers.

"Yes, and this is Luke—"

"Matthias," Luke said. He winked at her.

"Nice to meet you both," Rick said.

"This only involves Ms. Gabriel," Juan said. "You can wait out here for her."

"Oh, he's coming with me," Alona said. She wrapped her arm through his. "He's my Guardian Angel."

"Okay?" Rick said.

"Right this way," Juan said.

They walked into the office meeting room. Once inside, the four of them sat at a large oval table. There were notebooks where both Rick and Juan sat.

"I filled Rick in on your situation with the charges against Eduardo Muñoz and Jorge Villa being dropped due to their sudden deaths."

"Can you explain how you ended up in the warehouse where these men were killed?" Rick asked.

"I was abducted, along with my coworker and your sister-in-law," she said.

Rick and Juan glanced at each other.

"Didn't Elena tell you?" she asked.

"Uh, no," Juan said. Rick wrote some notes.

"Did you know Eduardo Muñoz and Jorge Villa were both present in the warehouse?" Juan asked.

"No. Everyone I saw, with the exception of the demon, wore masks."

"Demon?" Rick asked.

"Yes. He was the sixth person but I'm sure you didn't find him there."

Luke took her hand and held it.

"How did you manage to escape with five people found dead in the same office you were held in?"

"I felt threatened, so I defended myself. Each time I tried to leave another person would show up."

"In what way did you feel threatened?" Juan asked.

Alona sat forward, still holding Luke's hand. "The first time, one of the men wearing a mask slapped me across the face, nearly knocking me off my seat. The second time, the demon threatened me that if I didn't work for him, he would take the souls of my friends."

Juan gave Rick a sideways glance.

"What makes you call him a demon?" Rick asked.

"Because he *was* a demon. All those men worked for him and did what he told them to do. They no longer had souls."

"Have either of you seen the video footage from the office cameras?" Luke asked.

Juan jotted down some notes. "No, we haven't," Rick said. "We'll check into that."

"Did you know Carlos Guttierez?" Rick asked.

"No. Who is that?" Alona asked.

"Carlos Guttierez also worked for A-Z Security Company. The same people from the warehouse," Juan said.

"Was he with the others?" Alona asked.

"No, Guttierez was found dead in a parking garage downtown," Juan said.

"What makes you think I had anything to do with that?" she asked.

"You were seen leaving the garage shortly after the man appeared on scene," Rick said.

"So, you've seen those tapes?" Luke asked.

"Just what was put out on the news," Rick said.

"Then you must have seen him threaten someone with a gun?" Alona asked.

Rick glanced at Juan.

"I defended myself and my coworker. What do you think he was going to do with the gun?"

"Did the police find any fingerprints tying these two incidents with Alona?" Luke asked.

"The only fingerprints were those of the deceased," Juan said.

"Look, if we're going to defend you, Alona, we need to know everything. The police think of you as a suspect in the warehouse crime."

"The only crime there was our abduction and the threats to our safety. Everything else was self-defense. According to the Constitution, I'm allowed to defend myself. I just choose not to use a gun. The end result would have been the same had I chosen to use a gun."

"How did you do it, then?" Rick asked.

"Do what?"

"How did you kill those men?" Rick asked.

Luke squeezed her hand. "Do you know what a Nephilim is?" he asked.

Rick shook his head. "No," said Juan.

"Nephilims are half angel and half human. They can do things humans can't, plus they are super strong," Luke said.

"What has that got to do with this case?" Juan asked.

"I am a Nephilim," Alona said. She stood up and demonstrated how she could grow taller and stopped at ceiling height. She reached out to Juan and put her hand around his neck. "I can grow twice this size if the ceiling wasn't here. And if I put a little pressure on your neck, you would be dead."

Rick jumped out of his seat. "What in the hell?"

Alona released Juan and returned to her normal size. "I can move very fast and become a blur to the cameras." She demonstrated by moving around the room.

Juan scratched his head.

"Alona has been fighting bullies and crime all her life,

but what she fought in that warehouse was evil. The demon escaped that afternoon, but we finally captured him last week. He's now serving an eternity in hell where he belongs," Luke said. He stood beside Alona. "Life is a spiritual battle, on a daily basis. I'm working with Alona to teach her how to defend herself in human ways. If defending yourself against known criminals is a crime, then the system is broken," Luke said.

"Do you have any more questions for me?" Alona asked.

Rick glanced at Juan. "I think we're good for now," Rick said.

"Yes, if we need anything further, we'll call you," Juan said.

"Good. Elena and Pete know all the details of the warehouse incident and the demon incident at my shop," Alona said.

"Good day, gentlemen," Luke said. He wrapped his arms around Alona and they were gone. He teleported Alona back to her shop.

"What just happened?" Rick asked.

"If my notes are correct, we were in the presence of angels," Juan said.

"How are we going to explain that to a jury?" Rick said.

"If we do our research right, maybe it won't go that far," Juan said.

"We need to talk to Elena and Pete," Rick said.

"And we need to see all the tapes and reports North Miami has on the warehouse office," Juan said.

"Yes, and the parking garage incident," Rick added.

Luke and Alona popped into the back room of her shop. Teresa was busy.

"Thank God you are here," Teresa said. "We just got three call-in orders while I had two customers here in the shop."

The last customer just left. Alona turned to Luke. "Would you like to run the register today, Luke?"

"Sure. I think I'm getting the hang of it."

"You're doing great, Luke," Teresa said. She pulled out some food-wrap paper to make the next sandwich on.

"I'll do the call-ins if you want to handle the walk-ins for now?" Alona said.

"Sure. This is an unusually busy Monday," Teresa said.

"I'll call a few hotels and see what's going on this week," Alona said. "I meant to do that the other day and forgot."

"If this keeps up, we'll need another food order like last week," Teresa said.

Before Alona finished the second sandwich, another customer came in. Then they all started trickling in one after another with barely enough time in between to breathe. Pretty soon, the two of them alternated between customers. With Luke's help, the three of them managed to stay busy until five, when a large call-in order for twelve sandwiches came in.

While Alona and Teresa made the sandwiches, Luke wiped down the tables and swept up front. When the customer came in, Alona took care of his order while Teresa started the cleanup in the kitchen.

"I noticed you aren't a regular. What brings you to the area?" Alona asked the customer.

"Oh, I'm part of a setup crew. There's a Comic Book

Convention later this week. We're here to set up the rooms for the panels at the hotel down the street. They told us you had great sandwiches," he said.

Alona put all the sandwiches in a large bag. "I wrote the names of the sandwiches on each wrapper. Did you need drinks?"

"No, we got that covered."

"What is a Comic Book Convention?" Teresa asked.

"A lot of people who sell comic books will be there as vendors. Then there are animated shows with these characters, so the voice actors show up and sign autographs. Then there are vendors who sell items related to the shows or characters. The panels are where the speaker talks about things related to the characters or comic stuff in general. Sometimes there's a band that plays music. People come to see these characters and buy items and they all dress up as some of the characters from these animated shows. It's really cool fun. You should check it out. It runs from Thursday to Sunday."

After Luke rang up the sale, the customer paid him and then left. Luke locked up while Alona and Teresa finished the cleanup.

As usual, they all walked to the parking garage together. "That Comic Book Convention sounds like fun. Maybe Renaldo will go with me to it," Teresa said.

Alona glanced at Luke. "Maybe we can check it out as well?"

Luke smiled. "Whatever you want is fine with me."

12

Chapter Twelve

By the end of the week, Alona was tired from the long days, but she was excited to check out the Comic Book Convention. Renaldo came in before closing and Teresa introduced him to Luke and her.

Since the convention was down the street, the four of them walked to the hotel where it was held. Teresa had called about tickets earlier and there were tickets available at the door.

Alona and Luke held hands while they walked behind Teresa and Renaldo. She watched them hold hands and whisper to each other. She thought about how young love was cute to watch from a distance. Even though she had centuries of experience, with Luke, everything was new and different. She smiled at the thought of being alone with him later tonight. Each night was exciting because she never knew what to expect from him. But tonight, they would plan their wedding and honeymoon.

Once they bought their tickets, the four of them studied the map and schedule. People milled around in the entrance area doing the same thing.

"Since this is day two of this convention, why don't we do this panel," Alona said. She pointed to Comic Book Con 101 on the schedule.

"Yes," Teresa said, "then we can figure out what's going on." The four headed down the hall, searching for the room.

Alona did double-takes when costumed people passed by. The costumes were elaborate, but she didn't recognize any of the characters.

Luke elbowed her and pointed at someone coming toward them. It was a Jedi character walking with Yoda. She nodded and smiled. "You never told me what other voices you do," she said to Luke.

"Which voice do you want to hear?"

"Han Solo?"

He pulled her tight. "Maybe you need more scoundrels in your life."

"Oooh, that's good." Their faces were close. "I think I need just one scoundrel right now." She caressed his face. Before she could kiss him, she heard Teresa call out.

"Come on! We're going to be late!"

Luke took her hand, and they walked faster to catch up.

They sat together in the back of the room and listened to the speaker. He went over the things they could expect at the con, going on for about thirty minutes. After that, Luke and Alona decided on going to another panel down the hall. Teresa and Renaldo decided on a different panel.

"Let's meet near the entrance when you're finished," Alona said.

While they awaited the next speaker, Luke whispered in her ear. "I need to give you the sight so you can see spiritual beings."

"Okay. Will it hurt?"

"No," he laughed. He touched her eyes with his hand, and she glanced around.

"I'm seeing some shadowy figures," she said.

"I'm seeing them, too. Just be wary of the evil ones. I'm sure you can feel the presence of evil, right?"

"I think so. At least I can smell a demon."

They sat through a Star Wars panel and watched a room full of fans answer trivia questions. Afterward, they walked down the hall back toward the entrance area since they finished early. Alona found a bench and they sat there watching people in costumes walk by.

Luke sat up.

"What is it?"

He leaned close and whispered. "See those two bird-like creatures in blue?"

"Yes?"

"I've seen them before. And those aren't costumes."

"They aren't?"

"No. They are beings from another planetary system in the 5th or 6th density."

"Are we the only two who can see them?"

"I'm not sure. They can lower their frequency if they choose to."

"Interesting," she said.

A quick motion off to her right caught her eye. It was Teresa moving toward her. "Teresa!" she called out.

"There you are!"

"Where's Renaldo?" Luke asked.

Teresa swung around. "He was with me a moment ago."

She glanced around. Alona and Luke stood and walked toward Teresa. "Why don't you call him on the phone?" she said.

Teresa made the call. Alona glanced around but didn't see Renaldo anywhere.

"He's not answering."

"Try texting him," Luke said. He glanced at Alona. "Do you see him?"

"No. How about you?"

Luke shook his head. He checked the map. "The panels are on this side of the building and the Vendor hall is on the other side. Maybe we can split up and look for him?"

"Uh, no. I don't like the feeling I'm getting, and I don't want to lose you in this crowd."

Luke reached out and took her hand, giving it a squeeze. "I feel it, too," he whispered.

"Maybe we could wait a few minutes to see if he responds to my call or text and then go searching for him?" Teresa asked.

"Sounds good," Luke said.

After about fifteen minutes, Teresa began to panic. "Did he say anything to you?" Luke asked her.

"No. We were holding hands, and someone bumped into us. Then I saw you and realized he was gone."

Luke reached out and touched Teresa's shoulder. "I want you to picture the image of the person bumping into you, the way it happened, when you lost contact with Renaldo."

Teresa closed her eyes. Luke saw someone in a dark, hooded cloak bump into her, as if she wasn't there. "I saw him," Luke said.

"You saw Renaldo?" Teresa asked.

"No. I saw the entity that bumped into you. I'm not getting good vibes about it either."

"What do you mean?"

"Let's see if we can find him. We'll check every room on this side," Luke said.

The three of them walked down the hall searching for Renaldo. Luke checked all the men's rooms with no luck. The panels had already begun, so they stuck their heads into each room and called out "Renaldo Perez" with no luck. They made their way around to the other side and checked in the Vendor hall and the game room. They had no luck there, either.

"Check your phone again, Teresa," Alona said.

Teresa checked for text messages, then called him again. "It's going to voicemail. That's not like him, Alona. I'm getting worried."

"Let's report this to the authorities," Luke said.

The three of them went to the entrance and spoke to the personnel there. A security guard was called, and he came to speak to them. Teresa showed him a picture of Renaldo. "He's not answering his phone or texts," she said.

"Maybe his phone died, and he has no way to charge it?"

"Can I send you his image, so you'll know him if you see him?" Teresa asked.

The security guard was reluctant, but finally said yes.

"Should we also call the police?" Alona asked.

"I think it has to be 24 hours before they will start an investigation, unless he's got some medical condition," the security guard said.

Teresa glanced at Alona and Luke. "I just can't leave here without him. What should I do?"

Luke put his arms around Alona and Teresa. "Hang on."

In the next instant, the three of them were in an office. There were three others in the office. Alona realized it was Pete and Elena with someone else.

Luke stepped away from Alona and Teresa. "We need your help."

GUARDIANS

Chapter One

"My friend just disappeared before my eyes," she said.

"Have you contacted the police?" Pete asked.

"Yes, but she has to be missing for twenty-four hours to be considered missing," she said.

Elena stood and pointed to a comfy chair. "Have a seat."

The woman sat down facing Elena's desk and Pete sat beside her.

"Tell us what happened," Pete said.

Elena pulled out a notepad and wrote down what the woman said.

"We were at a Comic Book Convention down the street. We were sitting in a room where a panel had just taken place. Almost everyone was gone but me and Eva. We were trying to decide which panel to go to next when I noticed a movement off to my right, near some curtains. When I looked up, two very tall people stood there, wearing blue bird costumes. They glanced around the room and then walked away. Behind them, was a type of doorway with air moving around inside the door frame in a wavy motion. Eva jumped up and walked straight through the doorway and then, poof! The doorway was gone."

Pete Cummings stood up at the sudden entrance of three people into his new office in downtown Miami. "This is Luke—"

"Matthias," Luke responded.

"And this is Alona Gabriel and Teresa—"

"Martinez," Teresa said.

"And this is Crystal Stewart, our first client," Elena Cummings said.

"Welcome to Guardian Investigations," Pete said.

"Perfect name for your business," Luke said. "Sorry to interrupt, but we have a missing person to report."

"Did you report this to the police?" Pete asked.

"No, but the security guard said they couldn't help until he was missing for twenty-four hours," Luke said.

"See, that's what he said to me as well," Crystal said.

"Who told you that?" Alona asked.

"The security guard at the Comic Book Convention," Crystal said.

"Are you missing someone, too?" Teresa asked.

"My friend, Eva. She walked through a door and the door disappeared."

Luke walked up to Crystal and touched her shoulder. "What happened just before that?" he asked.

"These two people wearing bird costumes walked through the doorway. Eva jumped up and went through the door. Then the door was gone."

Luke stood up and glanced at Pete and Elena. "They were entities from another planetary system in 5th or 6th density. I think we're dealing with time portals."

"Time portals?" Pete asked.

"How can we help you?" Elena asked.

ABOUT THE AUTHOR

To keep up to date on Ester's book releases, and to get the FREE "Vaedra Chronicles" companion book, please join Ester's Readers Group at:

www.esterlopez.com

Follow Ester's Blogs at:

www.esterlopez.com

www.authorblogspot.esterlopez.com

Follow Ester on:

www.facebook.com/EsterLopezAuthor

or on Twitter at:

www.twitter.com/esterlopez1

And if you like the story, please leave an honest review at your favorite bookseller

You can also join Ester's Group Page on Facebook at Virtual Book Signing & Takeover Group

ALSO BY ESTER LÓPEZ

The Angel Chronicles Series

The Quest

Between Heaven and Earth

Golden Idols

Bailey's Irish Dream

Dark Demon

The Vaedra Chronicles Series

Genesis Saga

The Abduction

Revenge

Betrayed

Aftermath

Battle for Earth

Children's Books

The Adventures of Charlie and Ellie

Little Horses

Across the Big Ocean

www.ingramcontent.com/pod-product-compliance
Lightning Source LLC
Chambersburg PA
CBHW020334010826
48970CB00011B/654